BENDING

BENDING

and Other Dirty Kinky Stories about Pain, Power, Religion, Unicorns, and More

GRETA CHRISTINA

Pitchstone Publishing
Durham, North Carolina

Pitchstone Publishing
Durham, North Carolina 27705
www.pitchstonepublishing.com

Printed in the United States of America

ISBN 978-1634310079

"Craig's List," " Elephant Walk," " The Shame Photos," " Dixie's Girl-Toy Gets Spanked for the First Time," "What She's Not Telling Him," "Breasts," "Footstool," "This Isn't Right," "For No Reason," "Changing the Scene," "The Unicorn and the Rainbow," and "Open," all previously unpublished.

"View from the Fourteenth Floor," originally published in On Our Backs, April/May 2003. Reprinted in "On Our Backs: The Best Erotic Fiction, Volume Two," edited by Diana Cage, published by Alyson Books, 2004. Reprinted under the title "Humiliate Me" in "Best S/M Erotica: More Extreme Tales of Extreme Sex, Volume 2," edited by M. Christian, published by Venus Book Club, 2004.

"His Hands" and "Dear Marla," both originally published in Five Minute Erotica, edited by Carol Queen, published by Running Press, 2003.

"This Week," originally published in "Naughty Spanking Stories A-Z, Volume 2," edited by Rachel Kramer Bussel, Pretty Things Press, 2006. Reprinted in "C is for Coeds," edited by Alison Tyler, published by Cleis Press, 2007.

"Christian Domestic Discipline," "Penitence as a Perpetual Motion Machine," "The Rest Stop," and "Doing It Over," all originally published on Fishnet.

"Deprogramming," originally published in "X: An Erotic Treasury," edited by Susie Bright, published by Chronicle Books, 2008.

"A Live One," originally published in Penthouse, February 1997. Reprinted in "Penthouse: Between the Sheets," Time/Warner, 2001. Reprinted again in "Best American Erotica 2003," edited by Susie Bright, Simon & Schuster, 2003. Reprinted in "Paying For It: A Guide by Sex Workers for Their Clients," 2004.

"Bending," originally published in "Three Kinds of Asking For It: Erotic Novellas by Jill Soloway, Greta Christina, and Eric Albert," edited by Susie Bright, published by Touchstone/Simon & Schuster, 2005.

Cover design by Casimir Fornalski, http://casimirfornalski.com/.

For Ingrid.

Contents

UNICORNS AND RAINBOWS

RELIGION

SWEET STUFF

BENDING

Introduction

These are not nice stories.

These are not "erotica"—except in the sense that "erotica" has become the term of art in publishing for "dirty stories with some vaguely serious literary intent." These are not tender stories about couples in love making love. (Except for the one that is.) These are not sweet, gentle, happy stories about unicorns fucking rainbows. (Except for the one about the unicorn fucking the rainbow.)

A lot of fucked-up shit happens in a lot of these stories. Stuff happens here that is borderline consensual. Stuff happens that is not at all consensual. Stuff happens in which people manipulate other people into doing sexual things they don't want to do. Stuff happens in which people do sexual things they're ashamed of. Stuff happens in these stories that, if they happened in real life, I would be appalled and enraged by.

Stuff happens here that excites me to think about when I whack off.

I apparently have a very fucked-up sexual imagination.

But there is also love in these stories. Some of them, anyway. There is the love of long-term couples; there is the love of newly-discovered lovers; there is the love of friends. There is affection—between lovers, between colleagues, between strangers encountered on the street. There is respect: for love, for desire, for scars, for the complicated places where love and desire and scars overlap.

Above all, there is respect for sex itself. I think—I hope—that this respect underlies every story in this book. Beneath the excitement and the fear, the pain and the shame, the helplessness and the hunger, the danger and the love... there is always the idea that sex matters.

Since most of these stories are kinky, and since some people reading this may not be super-familiar with kink, I want to take a moment to talk about kinky porn.

Some of these stories are about consensual sadomasochism. They're about negotiated SM scenes between consenting adults, with safewords and limits and attention to safety. There's conflict in the stories, and mis-steps, and bad decisions... but fundamentally, what happens within those stories is consenting. They are attempts to express, in fiction, some of the things that consensual sadomasochists do.

And some of these stories aren't. Some of these stories are about force, and violation, and abuse of power. They are attempts to describe, not what consensual sadomasochists do, but some of the things we think about. They are attempts to describe some of the images that come into our minds when we masturbate, or have sex, or engage in consensual SM. They are attempts to describe some of the activities that some of us consensually act out with each other. They are fantasies.

And every single story in this book is consensual.

They're consensual because they're fiction. They're consensual because they're made-up. I consented to write them; you're consenting to read them. If you don't want to read this kind of thing, this isn't the book for you. I encourage you to put it down, and read something else.

It's funny. When it comes to things that aren't sex, people seem to understand this distinction. People get that enjoying spy novels doesn't mean you want to join the CIA; that enjoying murder mysteries doesn't mean you want to kill people; that enjoying heist thrillers doesn't mean you want to break into Fort Knox. People understand that it's fun and exciting to imagine things we wouldn't actually want to do—even things we think are immoral.

But for some reason, porn often gets held to a different standard. Depicting a fantasy of a sex act is often assumed to be an endorsement of that act. So let me spell it out: I do not endorse sexual force, abuse of power, rape, or any form of violation of sexual consent. I am vehemently opposed to them.

I am, however, unapologetic about the fact that I like to fantasize about them. If we have any freedom at all, it's the freedom between our ears: the freedom to think about whatever we like. And that includes sex.

Here's the deal with "Bending" (the novella that's the foundation of this collection). When I was writing it, I sent a draft to my editor, Susie Bright, who gave me this feedback (paraphrasing here):

"You have enough erotic treats for the readers. You don't need any more sex scenes. Focus now on fleshing out the story."

My reaction was to think, "What the fuck? This is porn. It's supposed to be about sex. So screw you. I'm going to write *more* sex scenes. In fact, I'm going to write nothing *but* sex scenes. I'm going to make the entire novella be just sex, from beginning to end."

So that's what I did. With the exception of a couple/few paragraphs, every sentence in "Bending" involves people either having sex, talking about sex, or thinking about sex.

And that's how the story gets told. Characters change, conflicts emerge, relationships develop, insights are gained, crises unfold… all through sex.

People often assume that I based the main character, Dallas, on myself. I really didn't: I am neither that brave nor that self-involved. But in a sense, of course I did. Dallas came from inside my head. It would be absurd to deny that. I sometimes think of Dallas as both my best and my worst self: shameless about her desires, fearless about asking for them, entirely confident that they matter—and every bit as confident that they should take top priority for everyone else in her life. She's a cautionary tale, and a heroine I aspire to be.

I've divided the other stories into five sections. There are stories about bad, bad ideas, people acting on impulse and letting the little head do the thinking. There are stories about force and power and the borderlands of consent, where the victims are technically free to leave but feel like they can't. There are stories about religion, where power and shame and violated consent get all tangled up with an all-powerful Judge, obsessed with our sex lives, who watches everything we do and will smack us down for it on a whim. And there are sweet stories about love and trust, intimacy and connection, people having sex that makes them entirely happy.

Oh—and then there's the story about the unicorn and the rainbow. Which I have no fucking idea where it came from.

There's overlap between these themes, of course. (Except the unicorn and rainbow one.) There's even one or two stories with all four themes at once. I love the places where love and impulse meet, and where shamelessness mixes with shame, and where power turns into helplessness and back again.

I hope you do, too. Enjoy!

BAD IDEAS

Craig's List

On her 24th birthday, she decided there were three things she wanted to do before she turned 25. Sexual things. All three involved taking stupid risks, putting her body into the hands of people she knew nothing about and had no reason to trust. All three involved Craig's List.

She knew she had to do them now. The older she got, the less reckless she'd become. She knew that if she waited until she was 30, she wouldn't be brave enough, or stupid enough, to try this. And she knew she'd always regret it if she didn't try.

The first one, she called Craig's List Roulette. She would go to the Casual Encounters ads, the Men Seeking Women section. She would pick an ad at random. No matter what it said, she would answer it. Unless she was literally and physically unable to comply with the ad's request, she would answer it.

She would use a random number generator, so she couldn't cheat.

She knew how stupid this was, how reckless, how dangerous. But she didn't want to be just another boring horny slut playing the personals. She wanted to set a new standard for sluts. She wanted to be the slut by which all other sluts measured themselves. Besides, reckless and dangerous was kind of the point. She wanted a real adventure—and in a real adventure, you weren't in control.

The ad headline read, "young, horny, need to get sucked." Perfect. Simple. Easy to take care of. She took a picture of herself, naked on her knees, and sent it with her reply.

She was at his dorm in twenty minutes. He wasn't as cute as she'd hoped—she thought he might have used a fake picture, actually—but that was okay. Weirdly, it was part of the charm. She closed his dorm

15

room door behind them, and dropped to her knees, thinking with a hard thump in her clit of how she had been manipulated, how she was being used. She dropped her head back and opened her mouth. He unzipped and pushed himself into her, and she opened wide and let him fuck her mouth.

He kicked her out politely when he was done, and she went home and masturbated for an hour and a half. She masturbated on her knees, with a dildo in her mouth and a vibrator between her legs. She kept thinking she couldn't possibly come any more... and then she would remember what she had just done, and her sore, tired clit would throb again, demanding just one more.

She was back on Craig's List the next day.

She hadn't expected that. When she first decided to do her three adventures, she'd assumed she'd play each of them just once. But she loved Craig's List Roulette. It was like slut boot camp. It was like an accelerated study program in human sexuality. It was like a multi-week intensive course in letting go. Her requirements got a little more re-strictive—the guy had to ask for something specific, he couldn't ask to do drugs together, he couldn't ask to do it more than once—but she stuck to the spirit of the game with remarkable discipline.

She landed on "Wanna watch me play with myself?" and was in a home-built weight room in a dingy garage, watching an oiled-up bodybuilder straddle his weight bench and stroke his cock, repeatedly murmuring, "You like what you see?", his eyes never leaving her face. She landed on "any one for a car date right now?" and was fumbling in the back of a Camry with a married ad exec, his hands groping at her tits, his cock pushing against her crotch through her panties, his breath pungent with weed. She landed on "Oral from behind" and was on her knees in a cheesy bachelor pad in the suburbs, a noisy tongue slurping at her pussy and occasionally, hesitatingly, perhaps even guiltily, slip-ping into her asshole. She landed on "Offering $$$ for pussy licking," and thought, "Sure, why not," and was on her back in a hotel bed with a tongue between her legs and three twenties on the bedside table. She thought she'd feel different after, and was surprised when she didn't.

She landed on "just give me a blowjob" and "Can a guy get a blow job please?" and "Looking for a woman in need of a facial" with perverse excitement. She loved how openly selfish they were. She loved how slutty it made her feel, how sordid, to get on her knees and open her mouth to a man who expressed no interest whatsoever in what she might need or want. She loved how it made her feel both purely sexual and purely invisible. And she loved feeling like the only woman in the city who would ever answer their ad. It made her feel extreme. Hardcore. Special.

She landed on "Looking For A Woman to Spank," and thought, "About fucking time." That was the first one—and the last—where she laid out her own guidelines. "I've never done this before," she told the guy. "I really want to. I want this to go well." The gentleman was older: in his early sixties, a little soft, a little frail, but patient and careful and grateful. He told her that she was beautiful, that she was bad, that he was going to teach her a lesson, that he was going to take care of her. He spanked her gently, until she wanted more than anything for him to spank her harder; and he spanked her harder, until she had no idea what she wanted anymore. He was the first one—and the only one—that she wished she could go back to. But that wasn't how the game was played.

She always felt a little guilty about the ones who just wanted to service her; the ones who ate her pussy or licked her feet or gave her long, drawn-out massages. It seemed like missing the point. But then she'd remember: This was what they'd asked for. When she lay back and let herself be taken care of, she was giving them the service they wanted more than anything.

It was disappointing sometimes. Naturally. There were clumsy men, smelly men, liars. But she kept the game up, a bit longer perhaps than she would have... because she was putting off the second one. She was a little afraid of the second one.

* * *

The second game, she called Motel Slut. It took a little more courage, more aggressiveness, since she had to place her own ad. Casual Encounters, Women Seeking Men. The ad read:

I am in the Star Motel on Broadway. I am in Room 314. I am naked. I will fuck the first man who shows up, in any position you like. Just tell me what you want, and don't talk about anything else. If the Do Not Disturb sign is up, you're too late—someone else got here first.

She placed the ad from her laptop in the motel room. The first man showed up in ten minutes. He was out of breath from running up the stairs. She hung the Do Not Disturb sign on the door, and immediately took off her robe. She was naked, as promised. "Tell me how you want to do it."

The man goggled. "Can we do it doggie style?

"Don't ask. Just tell."

He didn't seem to understand. But he went along. "Okay. Let's do it doggie style."

She gestured to the lube and condoms on the nightstand, and got on her hands and knees on the bed.

She played the image in her head again and again as he unzipped his pants and crawled between her knees. Opening the motel door to the stranger. Dropping her robe to show him her naked body. Saying nothing but a few terse words about sex. Putting herself silently on her hands and knees on the motel bed, and opening her legs so he could fuck her. She played the image again and again, as he pushed himself inside her. It was like a feedback loop screaming into her cunt. He wasn't a great lover—crude, a little clumsy—but it didn't matter. She felt like a character in a porno movie. She dropped into the feeling like a stone dropping into the sea.

Like Craig's List Roulette, she hadn't planned on doing this more than once. And like Craig's List Roulette, she was hooked after the first time. The next day, she did it again. She opened the motel door for another stranger; she dropped her robe; she lay on her back and spread her legs when he told her to; she let herself get fucked. And when he left, she took the Do Not Disturb sign off the door, and waited for the next one.

She did three guys that day. Seven the next. After that, she slowed down a bit: kept it to once a week, and usually no more than three or four in a day.

Some of them were simple. They just wanted a girl on her back with her legs open. And that was fine. It had a certain primal, meat-puppet charm. Some were more imaginative. And that was better. She liked being told to sit on the guy's dick and face away from him. To straddle him on a chair like a stripper and give him a lap dance that turned into a fuck. To lie back on the cheap motel desk, her butt scooted all the way to the end, her fingers spreading her cunt apart, her face turned to the wall. She liked being told to lie face down on the bathroom floor, her tits getting scraped by the cold tile as she got fucked from behind.

Sometimes it was hard. One of them told her, "I want to fuck you in the ass." She'd never done that before. Somehow, by a statistical freak, it had never come up in Craig's List Roulette. But the habit of compliance had become strong, and it didn't occur to her to say No. She gestured to the lube and the condoms on the nightstand, and said only, "Slowly, please. I've never done that before." And she got on her hands and knees on the bed.

It hurt a little. He wasn't as slow as he should have been. But that was kind of okay. Again, she pictured where she was, what she had done to get here, what she was doing now. She remembered that she was being fucked in the ass for the first time, in a sleazy motel room by a man she'd never met: a man she'd undressed for and offered herself to the moment he walked in the room. She remembered that she was face down on the bed and that her ass was being pushed open, too fast and too hard, because she'd invited any man who showed up at her door to fuck her any way he wanted. She remembered what a slut she was, that she'd asked for this, that she deserved this. She buried her face in the bed and whimpered: a genuine cry of pain and fear, blending imperceptibly with a moan of abandon.

She'd pictured her first time getting fucked in the ass a hundred times. She'd never pictured it happening like this. It was a hundred times better than she'd ever imagined.

She loved Motel Slut. And again, she kept the game up longer than she would have... because she was putting off the third one. She was more than a little afraid of the third one.

* * *

The third game, she called Pick the First.

It required a lot of courage. She was glad she'd put herself through Slut Boot Camp first. And it required strict honesty with herself. She couldn't rely on the randomness of a number generator, or the randomness of which man happened to be reading Craig's List at the moment she placed her ad.

In Pick the First, she had to read the ads on Craig's List. Casual Encounters, Men Seeking Women. She had to pick the first ad that turned her on; the first ad that made her want to masturbate. And she had to send them this email. She wrote it ahead of time, before she started looking, so she couldn't cheat.

I don't want to negotiate. I just want to do what you tell me. Please tell me what you want me to do, and what you want to do to me. Please tell me everything you can think of, now, so we don't ever have to talk about it again. If what you want is okay, I'll be at the Java Jive Cafe on 4th Street this Saturday at noon, with a black carnation in my hair. Please meet me there, and then take over.

It took longer than she'd thought to find the right ad. She considered "Submissive women needed for thick cock," but the poorly-lit photos of his torso and cock made her flinch with distaste. She thought about "arrive, bend over, submit, leave," but the scene he laid out stopped at sex and went nowhere interesting. She regretfully passed on "Cruel, Humiliating, Abusive and Sadistic": the headline make her clit jump like a kangaroo, but the ad was a letdown, with no juicy details, and an equivocating manner that put the lie to the promise of the headline. She kept an eye out for her spanking friend, but he wasn't on Craig's List that day. She saw "Brutal M Seeks Submissive W," and opened it. It read:

"I am a hard and unyielding man seeking a woman to whom I can do things. The things I want to do are not nice. I will want to use you sexually, humiliate you, hurt you, make you helpless. I will want you frightened, and suffering, and willing and compliant throughout. Am not looking for either brats or doormats. You should have desires, so I can deny them. You should have spirit, so I can break it."

It made her uneasy. To say the least. But it was the one she kept coming back to. The one she knew she'd be jerking off to. So bolstered by weeks of rigorous self-training in impulsive carelessness, she copied and pasted her pre-written reply, and hit Send.

He replied with a torrent of obscenity.

Implements he was going to use to beat her ass until she cried. Objects he was going to insert into her. Degrading positions he was going to force her into. Other men he was going to lend her to. He said he was going to wrestle her onto her back, pin her arms to the bed with his knees, and force his cock down her throat until she gagged. He said he was going to tie her hands so she couldn't fight, gag her so she couldn't scream, tie her legs apart, and whip her pussy before he fucked it. And then he was going to do the same to her asshole.

He said he was going to punish her righteously and ruthlessly for serious offenses. That he was going to punish her cruelly and unjustly for trumped-up offenses. That he was going to punish her for no reason at all except that he felt like it. He said he was going to make her spread her asshole apart for him with her hands, make her beg him to punish her by putting things inside it, make her apologize tearfully for being a bad girl while he did it. He said he was going to slap her face and call her a filthy whore while she sucked his cock.

He said he was going to rape her.

He went on for three pages. He apparently took "tell me everything you can think of" seriously. He finished with the words:

None of this is up for discussion. You will comply with all of it. You may show reluctance—I like reluctance—but you may not show resistance. Except when I rape you. When I rape you, I expect you to resist. I will see you on Saturday.

He scared the crap out of her.

She knew this was a bad idea. Even with her other Craig's List adventures, she hadn't done a third of the things he was talking about. She knew she was in over her head with this one. But she'd known that Craig's List Roulette and Motel Slut had been bad ideas, too. And they had been the best bad ideas of her life.

She put the date in her calendar for Saturday. And cleared the rest of her calendar.

View from the Fourteenth Floor

HUMILIATE ME

If you've ever wanted to humiliate another woman, here's your chance. Bring what you need on our first date—if we click, I'll want to do it right away. One night stands only.

Dana read the ad on Thursday. She masturbated furiously and then called the number. They made a date, and she spent most of Saturday making arrangements.

They met in a bar on Sunday evening. Dana arrived on time, and found Elizabeth already sitting in a corner booth. She was blonde, with an expensive haircut, dressed in a crisp white blouse and a single strand of pearls. She already had a drink in front of her. Dana settled into the booth. "So how long have you lived in New York?" she asked.

"Six days," Elizabeth said. "Look. Here are my limits. I don't like extreme physical pain, but keep it reasonable and we'll be fine. Psychologically you can do almost anything. My safeword is 'safeword.' And I mean it about the one night stand. After tonight, we're done." She took a sip of her drink. "You?"

Dana bit her lip. Elizabeth's tone offended her, made her want to slap the woman down. She noticed her clit thumping, and wondered for a moment if she was being played, if the girl was pissing her off on purpose. She stared rudely at Elizabeth's tits, and decided it didn't matter. "Your limits are fine," she said. "And mine aren't relevant to you. Do you want to do it?"

Elizabeth looked at Dana like she was appraising china. Finally she gave a small nod. "Yes. Let's do it."

"Good," Dana said. "That's the last word I want to hear from you until... well, ever, I guess." She strode out the door, leaving her drink untouched, and whistled for a cab. Elizabeth followed, eyeing her suspiciously as they got in the taxi. "Lester Hotel," Dana told the cabbie. "The one in midtown." She stayed silent all the way to the hotel, where she led Elizabeth to the fourteenth floor and pulled a key from her pocket.

Elizabeth looked around as the door closed behind her. The room looked untouched, except for an armchair sitting at an odd angle in the dressing nook off the bedroom. The decor was elegant and unpretentious, with tall windows that took up most of the outside wall. Dana switched on all the lights, switched off the one in the dressing nook, settled into the armchair, and began to speak.

"Did you know that every week, dozens of telescopes are sold in the city of New York? Hundreds even, on a busy week. Interesting statistic. Nobody seriously thinks all those people are stargazing in Connecticut on weekends. Everyone knows exactly what all those New Yorkers are doing with all those telescopes. And yet everyone goes on with their lives, in front of their open windows, as if they actually had privacy.

"Open the curtains."

She could see Elizabeth flinch before she obeyed. Good, she thought. This could work.

"It's Sunday night," Dana continued, "so a lot of people are home. And bored, and looking for something to do. When I scoped out the room earlier, I estimated about five thousand windows with a direct view of this one. Probably about fifty have telescopes. More if you count binoculars. So I'm guessing we've got anywhere from ten to thirty people in the audience tonight. Maybe more.

"Now take off your blouse and wander around the room. Act like you're a normal human being who's just changing for dinner, but keep turning to face the window."

Elizabeth stopped in her tracks. She turned from the window and looked Dana in the face, dismayed, her arrogance slipping off like a discreet partygoer escaping a bad soiree.

"Don't look at me," Dana snapped. "Face the window again. Now." Elizabeth complied, her shoulders slumping, and Dana went on, calmer. "See, I placed this chair very carefully. I can see you, and your reflection in the window, but people outside probably can't see me. So don't look at me again. I don't want our audience to know I'm here. I want them to think you're doing this on your own.

"I was going to build this up nice and slow, give you some time to get used to it. But now I don't think I'm going to. Strip down to your bra and panties, and start doing jumping jacks."

This was good, Dana thought as she crossed her legs. She could see Elizabeth squeeze her eyes shut as she wriggled out of her skirt and stripped off her shoes and pantyhose; she could see the reflection of the woman's blushing face as she tentatively began to jump up and down. She could see Elizabeth's butt jiggling through her panties, her breasts bouncing in her white bra, like a jiggle girl in a music video. She cleared her throat.

"Right about now," she said, "your audience should be figuring out that something's up. They're realizing that you haven't just forgotten about the curtains. By now they know you're doing this on purpose.

"Open the bedside drawer."

Elizabeth complied. She looked inside and cringed, arrogant revulsion arguing on her face with shame and disgrace. Dana hadn't picked the toys to be tacky on purpose: she just hadn't wanted to mess with condoms and stuff, so she'd picked up a few cheap things she could throw away. But now the choice seemed serendipitous. Inspired even. She loved the thought of making this arrogant bitch put these sleazy things into her body in full view of midtown Manhattan.

"So let's get started," she said. "Lay the toys out on the bed. Take off your bra and panties. Then lie on the bed with your cunt facing the window. Put the pillows under your head so people can see your face, and spread your legs."

She could see Elizabeth breathing hard. The woman was obeying, but she was doing it slowly, hesitantly, and Dana wasn't sure if she was genuinely scared or drawing things out on purpose. Either way was fine with Dana. She pressed her thighs together as she watched Elizabeth display her new toys and spread herself out.

"So we've shown them you're an exhibitionist," Dana said. "Now let's show them that you're a pervert. Put the ball gag in your mouth. Stick the buttplug in your asshole. And then spread your cunt lips apart with your fingers. Don't touch your clit. Not yet."

Elizabeth stared fiercely at the wall as she bit down on the pink rubber ball and fiddled behind her head to buckle the straps. She turned over to insert the buttplug, but Dana snapped her fingers. "No," she barked. "Stay on your back. I know it's awkward. That's what I want." She felt a warm glow in her stomach as she watched Elizabeth struggle, groping for her asshole with her feet in the air. She could see Elizabeth fighting to regain some dignity as she settled back into place; she could see that dignity slip away again as the girl remembered her instructions, put her fingers on her pussy lips, and slowly spread them apart. Dana paused for a moment to enjoy the view: the city lights, the wall of high-rise windows shining in the night sky, with Elizabeth's debased reflection superimposed over it all. She let Elizabeth lie quietly for a minute, let her exposure sink in. Then she spoke again.

"I notice you keep your eyes away from the window. You keep focusing on something else, or else you close your eyes. So look out the window now. Think of the people watching you, and look them in the eye."

Dana waited patiently as Elizabeth squeezed her eyes shut, shuddered, and reluctantly turned to face her reflection. She caught Elizabeth's eye and saw her whimper; her pussy clenched, and she pressed on. "Now take the dildo in one hand," she said, "and the ruler in the other. Stick the dildo in your cunt and fuck yourself. Every few strokes, pull the dildo out and smack your pussy a few times with the ruler. Then do it all again. And keep your eyes on the people watching you.

"Here's the picture they're getting. They see a woman who goes into a hotel room and puts on a free sex show. They see a woman who opens her curtains, strips, jumps up and down to get their attention, then opens her legs, puts a gag in her mouth and a plug in her asshole, and spanks herself on the pussy while she fucks herself. All for them to see. And they're looking you in the eye. You can't hide from them. They know who you are."

The dildo was a squishy plastic one, a lurid pinky-tan with prominent veins. She could see Elizabeth cringe as she slid it into her visibly wet pussy; she watched her flinch as she pulled it out, gripped the ruler, and gave her clit a few hesitant smacks. It was all gone now, the arrogance, the composure, the sense of entitlement. She had stripped the woman down to a trashy slut giving a free sex show to strangers with nasty toys from a corner porn shop. Dana took a deep breath and delivered the final blow.

"I'm leaving now," she said. "I have another hotel room across the street, with my own telescope. I expect you to keep up the show for another hour. You can do any nasty degrading thing to yourself that you like, but keep the ball gag in, and keep your eyes on the window. If I don't like what I see, I'm coming back, and you won't be happy about that." She paused. "If I do like what I see, I won't be back. In an hour you can shut the curtain and do what you want. The room's paid up for the night. Checkout's at noon. It's been lovely."

Dana dropped the room key on the floor and left Elizabeth on the bed, violating herself, alarmed, shivering, near tears. She whistled quietly as she shut the door and rode the elevator to the lobby. She caught a cab in front of the hotel, and told the driver to take her home.

His Hands

This is what she thinks about, when she thinks about him. She doesn't think about his eyes, like she likes to tell herself; or about his lips, like she'd tell her friends if they knew about him; or about his cock, like she tells him when she's in a good mood. She thinks about his hands.

When he wants her, it's always his hands that go first. Brushing lightly against her face. Sneaking up on her thigh. Massaging the back of her neck, and then inching down over her collarbones to entice her breasts. His hands are smart—smarter than he is, probably—and his hands are sweet when they want to be, and they can make her feel calm and drifty, safe and befriended.

But it isn't these nice sweet things she thinks about. His hands also do things that make her blush when she remembers, things that make her flinch and quickly look for something to stare at on the floor, convinced that anyone who sees her can read her mind. When she thinks about his hands, these are the things she thinks about.

She thinks about his hands pressing her against the wall, one hand pinning her shoulders, the other sliding up her skirt, pushing between her legs, reaching for her clit like it belongs to him. No, not like it belongs to him. Like a thief. Like he knows it doesn't belong to him and is taking it anyway.

She thinks about his hands pressing her thighs apart, again like a thief, like a catburglar, opening a window and climbing inside. She thinks about his hand on the back of her neck, his fingers coiling in her hair and tightening; she thinks about his other hand gripping her by the wrist, guiding her own hand between his legs, making her feel his swelling crotch. She thinks about his hands on her arms, shaking, impatient, maneuvering her body into place.

She thinks about his fingers spreading her lips open down there, prying her apart, exposing her clit and studying it fervently like he's reading her soul. When he opens her up like that, she feels like he is revealing her soul, like her soul has been hiding in her clit and he's discovered it at last: her true soul, the selfish one, the dirty one, the one that wants to quit her job and abandon her friends and family and spend the rest of her life on her back, on her hands and knees, pressed against the wall, with his hand between her legs.

She thinks he's a bad idea. She thinks she doesn't love him. She thinks that if she loved him, she wouldn't feel so dirty all the time. She thinks that if she loved him, she'd think about his eyes, his lips, even his cock, at least sometimes. She thinks that if she loved him, she wouldn't be spending every spare moment thinking about his hands.

She thinks about his hands. And finds her own hand knocking at his door.

Elephant Walk

"Yo! Anybody down here?"

Abby jumped up off the sofa at the booming voice. She thought she was alone in the house, and she'd been planning a lazy afternoon, drinking diet soda and watching soaps in the rec room. The first day of the last lazy summer before college. She planned to make the most of it.

But here was her big brother's best friend, lumbering down the stairs and hollering. She jumped up, and sat down again, and stretched out on the sofa, trying to act casual.

Donnie.

Oh, God.

Donnie poked his head into the rec room from the bottom of the stairs. "Hey, Squirt. Is Josh around?" He was taller even than she re-membered, and more muscled. And cuter. If that was, like, even pos-sible. He was wearing big loose shorts, and sneakers with no socks, and a short-sleeved baseball shirt unbuttoned and flopping open. He was staring at her with that dumb, big-mouthed grin, and she crossed her legs, then uncrossed them, then crossed them the other way.

"No," she said. "Josh's flight got delayed, he won't be here 'til to-morrow." She stopped for a second, then blurted out, "And my parents are gone, too."

Why the hell did I say that, she cringed. He doesn't care. God, I sound like an idiot. She waited for him to holler, "Okay, cool, thanks," over his shoulder as he pounded back up the stairs and out of her life again.

But instead he stared at her blankly for another second, like he'd just realized she was there... then lumbered into the rec room and flopped onto the faded Barcalounger. He took a gulp of her soda. "Really. Cool. So, Squirt, you're looking good. How's with you?"

He was actually talking to her. Like she wasn't just Josh's kid sister. Almost like he knew she existed. Which he hadn't for, like, eight years. And he said she looked good. She was suddenly self-conscious of her little sundress, the skinny straps that kept slipping off her shoulders, the thin fabric you could almost see through in the sun. She pulled her legs up under her, trying to relax, and said, "Oh, you know. Pretty good. Graduation was yesterday, so done with that, thank God. Now I just wanna chill out before, you know, college and stuff..."

"Yeah? Where you going?"

"Berkeley."

His eyes widened. "Really? Damn. You must be a brain. I had no idea."

"No—it's not—I'm not—" God, why had she said that? Now he was going to think she was stuck-up or something. She tried again. "I mean, I know Berkeley's all, it seems like, but it's really not—"

"Hey, it's okay," he laughed. "It's cool to be a brain. You'll probably make a million dollars." He took another gulp of her soda. "So, God, it's been a million years since I saw you. A year and a half, or what? You must be, like, two feet taller. You were such a little shrimp back then."

"Yeah, yeah. Late bloomer. Whatever." She hated thinking about that. Last in her class to get her period, last to get breasts, last to get everything. "I'm sick of hearing about it, if you want to know."

"I bet you are. Hey, Squirt, come here a sec"... and he reached out to the sofa, grabbed her hand, and pulled her into his lap.

She froze. He was acting all casual, like having his friend's kid sister sit on his lap was something they did all the time. But it was completely weird. She'd known him almost ten years, and she hadn't sat in his lap once. She'd have remembered. She sat perfectly still, her brain focused on the place where her back was touching his chest, and where the backs of her bare thighs were pressing against his legs.

But he was all casual, asking her all these questions like this was normal—"So what are you going to major in? Science, or English, or what? What made you wanna go to Berkeley?" He was even sort of listening to the answers, and she tried to pull her head together and not sound like a total idiot. "Any of your old friends going up there? God, remember how me and Josh used to give you kids so much shit? Hey, you still ticklish?"

She screamed even before his hands touched her belly. His hands jabbed and darted around her waist: she shrieked hysterically and tried to pull away, but he grabbed her around the waist and held her on his lap, tightening his grip with one hand as he made her scream and writhe with the other. "It's the Tickle Police!" he hollered. "You can't escape!"

It was almost normal, in a weird way. Donnie and Josh used to do this all the time: when they weren't totally ignoring her they were tormenting her, and the Tickle Police used to bust in on her and her friends all the time. But it was normal in an awful way. She hated being tickled, it seriously freaked her out. And it was totally embarrassing, too. She could feel her dress pulling up as she jerked around on his lap, screaming and trying to get away from his hands, and she thought she could feel his dick starting to get hard underneath her. Now she was embarrassed for him—she knew that guys hated walking around with their hard-ons—but he kept tickling her, even faster, and she struggled wildly, in a panic to get her belly away from his hands, crossing her legs tight and praying that she wouldn't pee her pants.

He stopped, out of the blue, and she collapsed and gasped for breath. "Jesus, Donnie," she panted. "What the hell."

"Oh, come on, Squirt," he joshed. "I'm just fooling around. For old time's sake. Hey, remember Elephant Walk?"

He stood up suddenly, dumping her out of his lap and onto the floor. He jumped up to stand behind her, and lurched over, plopping his hands on the floor in front of her. "Come on, Squirt," he coaxed. "Don't tell me you forgot Elephant Walk? Get up on my hands and feet, and let's go!"

This was weird, too. But in a completely different way. "Elephant Walk" was actually something they'd done before, a game her family used to play. The grownups and older kids would lumber around on their hands and feet, pretending to be elephants, and the little kids would put their feet and hands on the grownups' and get marched around the room. She'd done it a hundred times. She'd probably even done it with Donnie.

But this was different. She wasn't five now, she was eighteen, and it was weird. She scrambled up and put her hands and feet on his like he wanted her to, but she could barely fit underneath him, and his body pressed awkwardly against her back. She tried to curl up away from him, but she couldn't do it and keep her balance, and when he took the first step she stumbled and fell, pulling them both down in a heap.

He didn't get up right away. He stayed on top of her for a minute, breathing hard and crushing her into the carpet. Oh, my God, she thought, I hurt him, what if he messed up his knee again and can't play. But he sprang back into position and pulled her back up. "Come on, Squirt, that's not how you do it. Legs out, trunks in a row, let's go for a walk like the elephants go!"

She could feel his hips shifting against her bottom as he marched her around the rec room. She was totally embarrassed—on top of everything else, she could feel her short dress starting to ride up over her panties. And now she was pretty sure he did have a hard-on. She didn't want to embarrass him, she kept trying to wiggle away from it, but she couldn't do it and keep from falling, and the wiggling just made her dress ride up more. So she tried to hold herself as still as she could, and let him march her around the room, around the sofa and the card table and the ice hockey game. He lumbered them over to the Barcalounger, reared up his hands with hers on top of them, and slammed their hands into the cracked leatherette seat. "And, the finish line!" he crowed. "The crowd goes wild!"

She lay there gasping, trying to catch her breath, waiting for him to jump up and make some dumb joke. But he just stayed there, pressing her into the seat cushion, dramatically gasping for breath himself. She was suddenly aware of how big he was: he surrounded her, his chest pressing into her back, his massive thighs pressing her legs together, his hard thing pressed lightly against her bottom. He stayed on top of her for a minute, catching his breath. And then he started tickling her again.

But not like before.

It wasn't even tickling, really. It was slower, and lighter, and not as frantic. It made her wiggle and squirm like she was being tickled, but it didn't make her shriek and fight. It felt good. Weird, and hard to keep still, but good. And she still couldn't believe he was really here, hanging around just to horse around with her. She wiggled against him and pressed her back hard up into his chest, like she was fighting back from his tickles, but really wanting to give his hands more room to move... and wanting to get him to stay.

They stayed that way a while, his hands wandering up and down her belly, her back squirming against his chest. He drifted up for a moment to the bottom of her breasts, and she gasped and jerked away, and pressed her breasts into the seat cushion. He slipped his hands back down to her belly at once, and she immediately regretted her reflex. Why the hell did I do that, she thought. He's going to think I don't like him. He's going to get bored and take off. But he stayed where he was, and he kept his hands wandering around on her belly, and she wiggled again, backing her breasts away from the chair this time, trying to give him the hint that it was okay to try again. His hands inched back up to her breasts: she gasped again, but stayed resolutely in place, and his hands moved all the way onto her breasts, tickling lightly, his hips pushing lightly against her backside in a slow, almost imperceptible rhythm.

Oh, my God. She was making out with Donnie Willis.

She'd made out before. She'd gotten to second base, and even third for a minute or two. But it was always a guy she'd been dating, or had dated a couple of times anyway, and they were always kissing and stuff while they were doing it. This time she wasn't kissing him. She couldn't even see his face. It felt dirty, like one of those Victorian stories in that book her friend Donna had passed around. It felt dirty like that, and even sort of scary.

But Donnie was so familiar. And he was so cute. And he was so—he was Donnie. She was actually making out with Donnie Willis. Donnie Willis was touching her breasts and rubbing his thing against her, and okay, he wasn't kissing her, but so what. She couldn't believe he even wanted to talk to her, and here he was making out with her. Okay, so this was weird, but it was also pretty cool. Okay.

Her hips were wiggling now, brushing back and forth against his thing as he tickle-touched her breasts. His fingers brushed across her nipples: she jerked back against his hips, and he pinned her legs together hard with his massive thighs, squeezing firmly against her small body. Then he jerked his legs apart, and her own legs, which had been wriggling against their confinement, sprang open.

He pushed his knees between her legs at once, pressing hers even farther apart. She gasped as she felt his knees push in between hers, but he settled back in and went back to tickling her breasts as if nothing weird had happened. His thing was rubbing between her legs now, just through his thin shorts and her panties. Her panties felt wet, and the horrified thought flashed through her mind: Oh, God, maybe I did pee my pants. She held perfectly still, praying that he wouldn't notice.

He didn't seem to notice. His hands wandered away from her breasts and down to her bare thighs, tickle-touching up and down the backs of her legs. She was trying to keep still, but her bottom kept twitching up towards him when he touched her inside her thighs, and he kept touching her there again and again. Then he tugged at the hem of the short dress that was riding up over her hips, and pulled it up to her waist.

And it hit her, like a hundred doors in her head all slamming open at once.

They weren't making out. They were going to Do It. She was going to do it, for the first time. Right now. And it wasn't with a boyfriend at the end of a date—it was here, in the middle of the afternoon, doing it from behind on the Barcalounger in her rec room.

With Donnie Willis.

His hands were tickle-touching her bottom now, through her panties, slowly, like he was waiting to see what she'd do about it. She did nothing—she held perfectly still, frozen, letting him do it—and he moved his hand down between her legs and began touching her there, up and down, through her panties. She held still and buried her face in the Barcalounger. She couldn't believe this was happening, after all these years of wishing for it so hard it hurt, and it was so totally not the way she'd imagined it, not like this, all casual and out of nowhere and bent over the Barcalounger with her dress pulled up. But his fingers felt so good between her legs and she didn't want him to stop... and it was Donnie Willis, and she didn't want him to go.

He pushed his hand inside her panties then, and she gasped as his fingers touched her flesh. He started tickling her there right away, flicking back and forth up over her pee-hole while he tugged at her panties with the other hand. He couldn't get them down, she wiggled and tried to help him but her legs were spread too wide, so he took his finger away from her pee-hole and pulled at her panties hard with both hands. She felt a sharp snap of elastic against her thigh, and felt the torn fabric slip to the floor. She whimpered, embarrassed that he could see everything now—her naked butt, and down between her legs where she was all wet, and everything.

She started feeling like she had to pee again. His fingers were rubbing up high near her pee-hole, and it felt hard and urgent down there. A weird hard shiver went through her, starting in her pee-hole and making her whole body twitch, and she clenched her fists tightly and squealed into the seat of the chair, trying to muffle the sound.

He stopped touching her and pulled back. Oh, God, she thought. What did I do. I did something wrong. He reached into his pocket: she could hear something rustling, like a candy wrapper being opened, and the light dawned. Thank God, she thought. I didn't screw up. Then: Thank God he has a condom. Then: Fuck. I totally would have let him do this without one. What is wrong with me.

He fumbled with himself for a moment, then pushed his hips against her. He had pulled down his shorts, and the touch of his naked skin against hers was like a slap in the face. He rubbed his thing between her legs for a moment, and then start jabbing it against her, trying to find his way in. She tried to open her legs wider, trying to help him, but she was pinned against the chair and couldn't move. All she could do was hold still and let him do it. He kept jabbing his thing between her legs, grunting and sweating and poking his thing up and down. And then it pushed in.

It hurt. She yelped and yanked her head up, and he grabbed her breasts and squeezed them, and pushed in a little more. She was being stretched too hard, pulled apart, like that time her gym teacher made her do the splits all the way even though she said it was hurting. She tried to hold still and relax, but he pushed in a little more, and she flinched in his arms and began to squirm. He gasped, and squeezed her breasts hard, and shoved her torso hard into the seat cushion with his full weight on top of her, pushing her breasts hard into his hands, and pushing himself inside her.

She couldn't move at all now. He was going in and out of her: the pain was starting to pass, and she tried to push back against him, or wiggle her hips, or something—but she was pinned down against the chair, and her legs and hips were pinned up against it, and she couldn't do anything. All she could do was feel his thing sliding in and out of her, and his sweaty chest sliding up around against her back, and her breasts being flattened against his hands. She didn't know what she was supposed to do, or if she was supposed to be doing anything. He was grunting, and doing it faster, and in her head she kept saying: I am having sex. With Donnie Willis. Donnie Willis is having sex with me.

Donnie Willis is fucking me.

He grunted loudly then, and shoved his hips against her hard, pushing himself in deeper and holding it. It hurt again, just for a moment, and she squealed into the seat cushion, hoping he didn't hear her. She didn't think he did: he just moaned extra-loud, and jabbed into her sharply five or six times, and shivered, and went limp.

He slumped on top of her, breathing deeply. She was wide awake. She was intensely conscious of the dripping between her legs, the sweat pooling behind her knees, the shag carpet scraping her shins and the tops of her feet, the ticking of the clock over the card table. His body was draped heavily across hers, pressing her face into the cracked leatherette, and she struggled to get her breath. She wondered if he had fallen asleep. She wondered what this all meant: if he'd liked it, if he thought she was pretty, if she'd see him again, if he was her boyfriend now. At last he shook himself. "Holy shit," he said. "That was... Jesus."

He pulled out of her, and wadded up the condom into her torn panties, and shoved them into his pocket. "Listen, Squirt... your brother doesn't have to know about this, right? He'd be all... I don't know. Let's keep this between us, okay?"

Oh. So that's what it meant.

"Sure," she said. "Okay. It's cool. Whatever."

He slid up his shorts and stood up. "Hey, listen," he said. "You going to be around for the summer? You wanna give me your cel number? Shoot me a text, the next time your folks aren't around?"

She pulled her sundress back down over her hips, and curled up into the Barcalounger. She picked up her soda can and rattled it. It was empty.

"It's good to see you, Donnie," she said. "You should probably go."

The Shame Photos

Here's how it begins: a photographer, and a woman in her thirties or early forties. He is a porn photographer who sometimes does other professional work; she is a professional woman who sometimes looks at porn photos. They meet in some business capacity: a conference, or a corporate shoot. They talk. His camera is on the hotel bar next to their untouched drinks.

"No, it's not that," she says. "I like your photos. They're good. They're very hot. It's just..."

"What?" he says. He's defensive, a little prickly, and also more than a little curious. Apart from critics, not too many people tell him to his face what they think of his work. Or what, precisely, it is that they want from their porn and are not getting. This could be illuminating.

"Well," she says. "You have these lovely photos of these—scenarios. The women licking someone's shoes, or dressed up like ponies, or what have you. But they always look sort of—posed. The faces are all wrong. They're too relaxed, too composed. For the things they're doing—it's all wrong."

"What do you want to see in their faces?"

She doesn't hesitate. "I want to see shame."

"Say that again."

She blushes a little. His voice is friendly and curious, but there's a hint of command in it, and it shifts her over a bit from feeling like a calm, objective critic into feeling the topic a bit more personally. But she goes on. "I want to see shame. When I look at a photo of a young girl on all fours with a plug in her ass licking her mistress's boots, I

39

don't want her to look like a bondage model who's doing her job. I want her to look like a young girl who's being humiliated. Like those dirty Japanese comics, but for real. I want her to look frightened, and powerless, and ashamed of herself. I want her to look like she doesn't want what's happening, and like she feels somehow that it's her fault, and that she deserves it."

"Hm," he says. "Fascinating. Tricky, though. How would you make that happen? Pro models tend not to be ashamed of what they do. And if they'd be ashamed to do something, they just don't do it. How would you get that look?"

"Well. You could do a couple of things." She's clearly thought about this at length. "You could get pro models, but pay them extra to push their boundaries a little, do the things they don't normally like to do. Or else... you could go with amateurs. Lifestyle people from the scene. Put out the word that you want to do a book of people pushing their limits, doing things they said they'd never do. Acting out the fantasies they're embarrassed about. You're a big enough name in the scene. I bet you'd get plenty of volunteers."

"Intriguing." He means it. His mind is going off in a dozen directions at once, and his dick is starting to throb. "So... what kinds of scenes would you like to see in a book like that?"

She shrugs. "Oh, the particular scenes don't matter so much. I mean, of course I have favorites. But that's... what matters more is that look of shame. That's what I want to see. You could call it The Shame Photos. I bet you'd sell thousands."

He shakes his head. She's steering the conversation back to what she wants from him, like a commission, and that's not where he wants to go. He wants to take this on a different path, the path that steers her over the cliff. "No," he says. "Let me rephrase. If you were to model for a book like that. Hypothetically. What are some of the scenes that you would do. Tell me."

Again, that slight note of command in his voice. Again, the grammatical shift, from asking her questions to telling her what to say. Her clit is twitching, and she can feel her self-possession start to crumble under her feet.

"There are so many…" She's procrastinating. It's always hard for her, that top- of- the- rollercoaster moment when she drops her dignity and lets herself fall… and she doesn't know if she's ready to do it here, in the hotel bar, with a man she's known for three hours.

"Start."

Her clit thumps hard. Her clit doesn't care if she's ready. She bows her head, and lets herself drop. "Enemas."

"Be more specific. What position? What are you wearing? Who else is there?"

"I'm naked. I'm on all fours, with my knees apart and my ass in the air. The room is empty, walls and a ceiling and a floor: there's not even a pretense that this is a medical procedure. The person giving me the enema is dressed in plain clothing: no fetish outfits, no medical gear. They're giving me the enema, and they're also periodically stopping to fuck me in the ass with the nozzle. My ass is filled with water, and they slide the nozzle in and out. They're looking down on me with contempt. My face is on the floor, but it's turned towards the camera, so the camera can see how ashamed I am."

"Of course. Why are you there?"

"I'm there because I have to be. That's always why I'm there. Not because I'm being punished, though. Because I made a bad mistake and let people have power over me. Like I'm being blackmailed, or fell in with the wrong crowd, or something. I'm powerless, but it's still my fault."

"Good. Thank you. Tell me another."

Now that she's begun, it's easier to go on. Falling has become easier than not falling. "I'm in a brothel. Victorian, I think: the girls are all in corsets and bloomers, the men are in suits. I lost a bet, or made the madame angry or something, so they're going to make me do the things I always refused to do. They're going to make me get whipped, and then get fucked in the ass. The madame makes a game of it. She puts me on display at a special party: puts me on a stage with my skirt pulled up and my bloomers pulled down, talks me up to the crowd. Then she takes me from customer to customer, and makes me show them my bottom and beg them to whip me and bugger me. It's obvious that I'm frightened, and some of the men are put off by that... but some are excited by it. She gets a good price.

"She goes into the room with me while it happens. She holds my wrists while he puts the money on the nightstand. She bends me over the bed and holds me down, while he pulls up my skirt and pulls down my knickers. He's made me cover myself again, so he can have the pleasure of exposing me for himself. It frightens me, and it fills me with shame. I've shown my bare bottom before, dozens of times, but never like this, never so helplessly, never so totally at the mercy of someone who's going to show me none. She holds me down, while he whips me, cruelly, brutally, and then forces his cock into my ass. I scream and cry and beg him to stop, he has to know that I don't want this, but that just makes him do it harder. He likes it that he's hurting me, that he's making me cry. There's a photographer in the room, a pornographer who pays the madame to let him photograph the whores, and he takes dozens of pictures of me while I'm being held down by the madame and my ass is being whipped and raped."

"Jesus," he says. "Fuck. More."

"Yes." The next one drops into place as smoothly as a moving part on an assembly line, and she doesn't even consider not telling him. "My pants are being pulled down, forced down, by a gang of three or four men. Young men, college age maybe. I'm struggling, but they're stronger than me, it's not even hard for them. One of them has my hands, one of them has grabbed me around the waist and is groping my tits, two of them have my legs and are unbuckling my belt and pulling down my pants. I'm struggling, but they're laughing at me. I don't know what they're going to do to me."

"Are you screaming for help?"

"Yes. I'm screaming and struggling. But we're in an abandoned warehouse or something. Nobody can hear me. I'm struggling, and I'm helpless, and they're laughing."

"What do they do?"

"I don't know. It doesn't get that far. All I think about is the four of them ganging up on me and pulling down my pants."

"Think about it," he insists. "You said you don't know what they're going to do to you. What are you afraid they're going to do? How are they going to shame you? Tell me."

She shivers. She's never gone there. She doesn't want to go there. But she's been telling these stories, and now she's in that place, where it feels like she doesn't have any choice, where it feels like she has to expose and humiliate herself when she's told to. She opens that door in her mind, and answers without hesitation, letting the words tumble out as the images pop in. "Probably they take turns fucking me in the ass. All of them, one after the other, while the others hold me down. Pin my hands down to the floor, and force my legs apart and pin them down. Force their cocks hard into my asshole, while I cry and beg them to stop. Maybe they tie my hands behind my back when they do it, or whip me with my belt. Maybe they wrestle me onto my hands and knees and force their cocks into my mouth, pull my hair and hold my head in place so they can get deep down my throat, with my pants still pulled down around my knees. And there's another one there with a camera, and he takes pictures. They force my ass cheeks apart, so he can take pictures of my asshole. And they force my head to face the camera, so everyone will know who it is. Who I am."

She stops. She's not sure that's it. This image is intense, it's making her squirm, but she's not sure it's right. She stops, and starts again. "Or maybe... maybe they just pull down my pants. And just look. And maybe touch my bare ass, just lightly, just enough so I'm aware of it. Maybe this isn't about gang rape. Maybe this is just about forcing my pants down. Forcing my bare bottom on display, for them to look at against my will, for as long as they want. And taking pictures. They take pictures of themselves pulling my pants down and exposing my ass and spreading my asshole apart, while I struggle and try to stop them. They take pictures of my bare ass, and my face."

He can see the picture in his mind. He's framing the shots while she talks, and his hard cock is getting harder, like it always does when he starts framing a new photo set. "That's good. That's really good. Tell me another one."

She doesn't want to be telling him this in the hotel bar. She wants to tell him this someplace where they can do something about it. She wants to tell him this on her knees. She wants him to tell her to act out the scenes she's describing: to strip naked and raise her ass in the air for the imaginary enema, to dress up like a Victorian whore and give her ass to the imaginary customer, to pull her pants down while she struggles against the imaginary assailants. She wants him to tell her to spread her asscheeks wide open for his camera, her own hands standing in for the hands of the men humiliating her. She has a hundred of these stories. She could spend a week telling them. She could spend a lifetime acting them out.

She knows now where this is going. In the back of her mind, she is already calculating what she'll have to do if it happens. How she'll keep her job when the book comes out. If she can't, what job she could get instead. Maybe she could work for one of the fetish publishers. They could use a good marketing exec.

She shakes her head. "Please," she says. "Not here. Please don't make me tell you here."

He's startled at her refusal. Then he looks at her face—pink cheeks, bowed head, pleading eyes—and he gets it. He can be a bit thick about these things sometimes, but he gets it. It's not a refusal. It's an invitation.

His studio is too far. An hour from here. Much too far.

"Get a room," he tells her. "A suite, here in this hotel. Here's my card, it has my cel number on it. As soon as you get to the room, call me. And don't do anything else. Just sit on a chair, and fold your hands in your lap, and wait."

He sees the shift in her face: the drop to the next level, from the humiliating acknowledgment of her fantasies to the humiliating need to make them real. He picks up his camera, and snaps a photo of her face. He knows it probably won't come out—the lighting in the bar is all wrong—but he wants to seize the moment. He wants to do this, and he wants to start now.

She flinches from the snap of the camera. "Go," he says. She stands up straight and strides out of the bar. She looks back at him, and at the revolving doors to the street outside, and walks to the registration desk. "I need a suite for the night."

FORCE, POWER,
AND MESSED-UP CONSENT

This Week

Here's what it is this week. A girl, a college student, is being spanked by her college professor. She's young, nineteen or twenty, young enough to be in college, but old enough to have some sexual knowledge. He's older, of course, probably in his forties, dressed casually but with dignity, a trim beard with a hint of gray. She is dressed, not in the schoolgirl outfit of porn cliché, but in regular modern clothing that merely implies the schoolgirl look: a short skirt with a flare, a simple blouse, white panties. The white panties are important. She is bent over his lap with her skirt pulled up and her panties pulled down, and he is spanking her with his hand.

Here's how they got there. I think of the girl as the instigator of the scenario. I think of her sitting in this man's class: admiring him, becoming excited by his ideas and his authority and his ease with his body. I think of her feeling flustered in his presence: not stupid, but young, and acutely self-conscious of her youth and her limitations. And I imagine these feelings coalescing into the simple image in her mind, the lap and the bare bottom and the hand coming down again and again. I think of her, not coolly deciding to act on her thoughts, but doing it impulsively, not even entirely consciously; just coming to him after classes for help and advice, putting herself in his path, waiting to see what happens next.

Now. I imagine her going to his house after a test, a test on which she had done fine but could have done better. She goes to his house, dressed only somewhat on purpose in the short skirt and simple blouse and white panties. She goes to his house, apparently upset about her less-than-ideal test score, telling him that she clearly needs more help. She works herself into an agitation, a frustration about her academic performance that even she half-believes. At the same time, she's deliberately, or semi-deliberately, being provocative, displaying her body, putting herself in poses both seductive and submissive. She talks about how lazy she is, how little self-discipline she has, how she needs external discipline to succeed—and she drops something on the floor and turns away from him to pick it up. She says she can't achieve her best unless she fears being punished, says a B+ grade isn't enough punishment to drive her to excel—and she bends over his desk to examine a knick-knack on the far side. She uses the word "punishment" again and again, and she keeps finding ways and reasons to turn away from him and bend over.

He's not an idiot. He's an adult, a middle-aged man of the world, and he can see what she wants. He wants it too; she's a lovely girl, she makes him feel powerful and wise, and the thought of bending her over his lap makes his dick twitch. At the same time, he's not an idiot. He knows how much trouble he could get into if he's guessing wrong, or for that matter if he's guessing right. So he's careful. He asks her if she wants his help, if she wants him to provide this external motivation she's missing, to give her the punishment she needs when she fails to reach her potential. She breathes a deep breath of relief and excitement, says yes, please, can he help her. He asks again: are you sure you want this discipline, are you sure you want to be punished for not doing your best, are you sure you want me to do it. She begins to pace around the room, agitated and anxious, saying yes, yes please, that's why she came here, this is what she wants.

He looks at her face, steadily, until she stops pacing and looks at him back. They're no longer speaking in code.

Do you want this, he says. Do you want me to punish you.

She nods. She can't say it out loud.

Alright, he says. Come here.

She walks over and stands next to him. He pats his lap; he can't say the words either, and he needs her to make the gesture on her own. She stares at his lap, and at his hands, and she awkwardly kneels on the floor and crawls over his knees.

He's done this before. Not often, but more than once, and he knows what he's doing. He pulls up her skirt, not slow and sexy, not rough and impatient, but deliberate, matter-of-fact, getting the job done. He waits for her breathing to relax, then puts his hands on her waist and pulls down her panties. He moves a bit slower this time, but his manner is not teasing or sensual; the slowness is methodical, patient, done with calm authority. He looks at her bare bottom, listens to her breath, waits.

He doesn't caress her—this isn't about that—but he does rest his hand on her bottom. She flinches, then realizes that he hasn't started yet, and tries to relax. He waits again. And then he begins to spank her.

His first blow is a real one. Not extreme, but she knows right away that she's being spanked. He waits, and delivers another blow, exactly the same. And then he begins to spank her in earnest. The spanking is slow, she can feel it each time his hand strikes her bottom. She begins to squirm; she's embarrassed now, self-conscious about what she's doing and how she must look, a grown woman being punished on her bare bottom like a child. And it hurts, it's hard now and it hurts, she wasn't expecting that. But she can't bring herself to say anything, she'd feel like a fool just quitting in the middle... and now it's lighter, and she thinks she can take it a little longer.

He says nothing. He concentrates on the spanking, watches her body, listens to her breathe. His cock is getting hard, it's telling him to squeeze her tits and then spank her as hard as he can; but he ignores it, tells it to be content with her warmth and her wriggling, and he centers his attention on just how hard he's spanking her, and what exactly she's doing about it.

She's squirming harder now. She feels how warm her bottom is getting, she can picture how pink it must be by now. She's getting agitated, and confused. The hard ones make her flinch and curl up—but the light ones give her time to think, and to feel: how small she is, and how flustered; her fear of the next really hard one; her uneasy frustration when the hard ones stop; her excitement; her shame at being excited; her hips wriggling against his lap. A good hard one comes down out of nowhere, and she cries out in relief and arches her back.

He still says nothing. He looks carefully now at her arched back and clenched fists, listens to the change in her voice. He stops, pulls his hand up high, and gives her five hard smacks, very hard, as fast as he can.

He listens as her cries of outrage subside into gasps. He considers starting again; he considers giving her a comforting pat on her pink bottom; he considers putting his hand between her legs. He's pretty sure he could do any of these things, and she'd respond. But he's nervous now, and doesn't know how far he wants this to go. So he pulls up her panties, carefully, not touching her skin. He pulls her skirt back down over her bottom, and then puts his hands behind his back.

She scrambles to her feet right away, looks down at the floor, her face red. She mumbles something—"Thank you, Professor," he thinks—and waits expectantly. "Good," he says. "That was very good." She stares at the floor for a moment, then scrambles for her things, mumbles "Thank you" again, and scurries out the door.

Here's what happens next. They meet once a week at his house. They don't discuss it, they don't make a plan; she just shows up at his door the next week at the same time, as if they had an appointment. She puts down her things, and she tells him about her schoolwork, the week's successes and failures. He congratulates her on her achievements, and then he analyzes her failures, explaining exactly what she did wrong and why it matters. And then he pats his lap.

It always has to be a punishment. She can't simply walk in the door and say "Okay, let's get to the spanking." And neither can he. They can't quite acknowledge what this is, they find it easier to think of it as instruction, discipline. Anyway, it's more exciting this way. So he begins to write tests, every week, just for her, tests for her to make mistakes on. She's a bright girl and she wants to please him; so he has to make the tests hard, hard enough that she'll miss at least one question and will need to be punished. She takes the tests very seriously, studies hard for them. She does, in fact, become a better student during this time, in all her classes, not just his. And she never misses a question on purpose. She would consider that cheating, and she is a serious student, appalled at the idea of cheating. She's always excited when he points out her errors and pats his lap; but she's always a bit disappointed as well, upset at herself for failing, and believing, at least somewhat, that she really is being punished, and that she deserves it.

As the weeks go by, they become more accustomed to each other. Their rhythm becomes more fluid, the ritual more detailed, the spankings longer and more intense. He begins to talk during the spankings, sometimes lecturing in detail on that week's failures, sometimes just chanting, "Bad girl! Bad! You can do better! You need discipline! You need to be punished! Punished! Bad!" He knows by now the words that set her off, the ones that make her whimper and arch her bottom in the air—and he knows the ones that make her freeze up. He knows how hard she likes to be spanked... and he knows how hard is just a little harder than she really likes, how hard is hard enough to make her feel that she's been bad, and is being punished for it.

As more weeks go by, he begins to ask if she needs any special punishment, something extra to make her pay closer attention. The first time she doesn't understand what he's getting at, she says no thank you, Professor, please just punish me. But she gets it later, alone in bed that night; and the next week when he asks again, she has her answer ready. Yes, she says. She fears that his hand isn't a hard enough tool for serious discipline, doesn't make her fearful enough or sorry enough for what she's done. She says she needs to be punished with something harder, something that will make her more afraid to fail, something to really hurt her and make her feel ashamed. He asks her to be specific—he always needs her to ask for it, always needs it spelled out—and she's learned by now to speak up. She asks him to please spank her with a ruler, wooden or maybe metal, or with his hairbrush. He tells her to fetch his ruler—the hairbrush is too personal for him—and she goes directly to his desk and takes it out of the top drawer. She knows exactly where he keeps it.

And as still more weeks go by, the special punishments become both more elaborate and more central to the ritual. The bare-bottom over-the-knee hand spankings, once the entire reason for them being there, now become prelude—neither of them will call it foreplay—to the special punishments she asks for each week. She asks him to spank her with a rolled-up newspaper. She asks him to make her say out loud what a bad girl she is while he spanks her. She asks him to make her get on her hands and knees and kiss the floor while he spanks her. She asks him to use the ruler to spank her between her legs. She asks him to keep spanking her until she cries.

She never asks him to fuck her. He never does.

The end of the semester draws near, and both of them are a bit at a loss. She has one more year before she graduates, and no more classes with him. She starts asking about her final exam; her questions are anxious, restless. He's pretty sure he knows what she wants. With some regret he begins crafting her final. He spends every spare moment on it. He knows it has to be perfect.

She comes to his house for the final, wearing the same short skirt and simple blouse and white panties she wore for their first lesson. He hands her the test, and she takes it without a word and begins immediately, working fiercely and steadily like a buzz saw. When she finishes, she hands it back and waits silently, tapping her fingers on her knee.

It's perfect, he says at last. No mistakes.

They both sit still, somewhat taken aback, sitting quietly together in the empty space that has just opened up. He guessed exactly right, this is what she wanted. But neither of them had thought about what to do next.

So, he says. No punishment today. You get punished for making mistakes. What do you get when you're perfect? Do you get a reward?

She doesn't know what to say. She'd imagined in detail how the test would go; a serious challenge, just barely within her abilities. She'd imagined her struggle to get through it, the rush of pride when he told her she was perfect. But she hadn't thought any further than that.

A reward, she says.

She could ask him to kiss her. She could ask him to fuck her. She could ask him to spend the afternoon feeding her tea and cakes and telling her how much he admired her. She could ask him to take off her shirt and play with her nipples, could tell him exactly how she wanted him to do it, and then she could make him get on his knees on the floor in front of her and lick her pussy. She could ask to sit in his lap, the lap she's been bent over so many times, and have him stroke her hair and tell her what a good girl she was. She could ask him to make her masturbate, make her lie back and spread her legs and show him how she did it, and then make her turn over onto her belly and keep masturbating, while he punished her hard on her bottom for doing it. She could ask him to give her all her special punishments over again, one after the other until she's weeping and raw, and then pin her down over his desk and push his cock into her ass. She could ask him to make the decision, to take the initiative, to for fuck's sake, just this once, not make her come to him. She could ask him to take her over his knee, and pull up her skirt and pull down her panties, and spank her bare bottom with his hand one more time.

I'm getting all A's this semester, she says. Every class. I think I'm going to make the Dean's list. And I got a special summer internship, a really good one. She tells him the professor she's interning with, and he's impressed, and a little jealous. That's great news, he says. I'm really pleased to hear it.

A reward, she says. I don't know. Let me think about it. She gathers her things, says, "Thank you, Professor," in a clear voice, and quietly leaves, shutting the door behind her.

Dixie's Girl-Toy Gets Spanked for the First Time

She is doing it to please Dixie.

She would do anything to please Dixie.

She is in Dixie's apartment. She is getting ready to be pull down her panties and be spanked by a lover, for the first time in her life. It's going to be videotaped. The video is going to be sold.

Dixie is there with her, of course. So are two camera guys. A lighting guy. A sound guy. A couple of gofers. The director. Another actress, for some reason.

She doesn't want to do this. She is frightened, and embarrassed.

But Dixie wants this.

So she is doing it.

* * *

She met Dixie at a party about four months ago. A real live porno star. A beautiful one. And one who liked girls. It took her the whole party to work up the nerve to say "Hi."

Dixie looked her up and down. Dixie said "Hi" back.

And she was lost.

Dixie was her first lesbian lover, just about. Dixie was older. Dixie was more experienced. Dixie was famous. Dixie was so beautiful, it hurt to look at her.

So she was lost. She was like a puppy with a distracted, not very nice mistress. Ecstatic when she got praise and attention; anxious and desperate to please when she was ignored or snapped at. She came over when Dixie called. She stayed away when Dixie didn't have time. She rolled on her back and spread her legs when Dixie was horny.

She would have done anything to please Dixie.

What happened was her own fault, really. That's what she told herself after. Dixie almost never asked her about herself, almost never asked what she liked or what she fantasized about. So when Dixie asked her what kind of pornos she liked, she got too excited, and said too much. "I like to watch... well... are you sure this is okay? I've never told anyone this. Okay, this is embarrassing, but—I like to watch spanking videos. I'm not saying I'd ever want to do that stuff myself," she added, too quickly, "but since you asked what I like to look at... well, that's it. Just to look at."

Dixie laughed. A boisterous laugh, friendly even, with only a hint of contempt. "You mean you've never been spanked? You're a spanking virgin? Jesus, how old are you again? That's right. I keep forgetting how young you are. But... Jesus. Never?"

So now she felt doubly ashamed. Ashamed of liking to look at spanking pornos... and ashamed of being so young and stupid that she'd never even been spanked before.

"Hey, we all gotta start somewhere," Dixie went on. "Tell me, what kind of spanking pornos do you like to see? We can do something with this, I bet."

She had no idea what Dixie meant by that. But for once, it sounded like Dixie was going to do something for her. Was Dixie going to watch spanking pornos with her? Was Dixie going to take her to one of those parties or private shows she'd heard about, and let her watch somebody get spanked? Was Dixie—she couldn't dare think about this, it was too tantalizing and too terrifying to think about for more than a few seconds—was Dixie going to spank her herself?

So she told. Her face getting redder and redder, she told Dixie the kinds of spanking pornos she liked to watch. The ones where a young girl gets spanked by an older woman: a teacher, a nun, a school principal, her mother. The ones where the girl gets spanked in front of her friends, or her sisters, or in front of the class. The ones where she gets spanked by hand, and then with something else: not with the leather SM toys, but with something ordinary, a hairbrush, or a yardstick. Not the ones where the girl is sassy and talks back, but the ones where she's scared. The ones where she's ashamed. The ones where she cries.

Dixie smiled. Dixie told her to roll over onto her back, and Dixie fucked her. Dixie fingered her clit and fucked her pussy, talking to her the whole time about spanking, and about helplessness, and about shame. She came hard, struggling, squirming away from the words in her ears and the pictures in her mind, and at the last moment clutching to hold on to them. She came, and she collapsed into a soft heap, and she gazed at Dixie in a gauzy blur of adoration. Maybe Dixie really did love her after all. Maybe this would be all right.

Dixie didn't call her for two weeks. Hysterical, freaked, convinced she'd driven her beautiful porn star away with her neediness and her sick desires, she waited for Dixie to call. She waited... and finally, after two weeks, Dixie showed up at her apartment unannounced.

"Okay. It's all set. My producer says they can definitely do something with this. Dixie's girl-toy gets spanked for the first time. Watch as Dixie turns the young girl's virgin bottom bright red. They can definitely market that. You're so young and fresh, people like that, and they love to watch cherries get popped. With spanking vids especially. If you look all scared and innocent, they love that, and the pro spanking models can never really pull it off."

Her stomach dropped through her cunt. Dixie wanted to spank her. And she wanted to do it for one of her videos. Dixie wanted to give her her first spanking... but she wanted to do it on camera, so she could sell it, so any guy who wanted could jerk off to it.

Her voice shriveled up in her throat. But her dismay must have shown on her face, and Dixie snorted in contempt.

"Jesus. I thought you were cool. I didn't know you were such a pussy. Okay, fine. If you don't want to hang, we don't have to hang. Whatever."

She was frozen. She couldn't say anything. Not Yes. But definitely not No. She had two impossible, unacceptable choices: being spanked and humiliated in front of strangers on video, and losing Dixie.

She nodded.

"Good girl," Dixie said. "It's all set up at my apartment. Let's go. Oh, you need to pick a porno name. And don't make it your first pet and the first street you lived on. That's lame. You know what, never mind. I'll pick one for you. How about: Cherry Bottoms. Don't worry about lines or script, just nod or shake your head when I talk to you. And make as much noise as you can. It's better if you make noise."

So Cherry Bottoms is in Dixie's apartment, about to get spanked for the first time, while a small crowd watches. She is dressed like a little girl, Britney Spears style. Dixie is dressed like a sexy June Cleaver. The end table next to the sofa has a neat set of household implements lined up: a hairbrush, a ruler, a wooden spoon. She is about to lose her spanking virginity, and she is selling it to her lover's porno producer. She is about to do the thing she has obsessed about with mortification and hunger for years, and she is about to do it with a camera—make that two cameras—capturing every moment, tying her to it so she can never escape.

They have started. Dixie is sitting on the sofa, scolding her for watching spanking videos on the Internet. She is naming all the ones Cherry told her about, and describing them in detail. Cherry squirms and blushes bright red. She could barely bring herself to tell Dixie about those. She doesn't want the whole world knowing about them. She's confused: usually in the vids they spank the girl for something stupid and made-up; but Dixie, apparently, wants to spank her for something real, something she's really ashamed of. Dixie asks her if she's ever been spanked before: she can't muster words, but she shakes her head vehemently. No. She never has. She knows this is just feeding the virgin-popping freaks, and it makes her queasy, but she knows Dixie wants the truth. No. She has never been spanked before today.

She is acutely conscious of all the eyes on her, and is feeling that consciousness multiplied by all the eyes that will be watching this video, down the weeks, and months, and years. Dixie has just told her to pull up her skirt and pull down her panties, and she is doing it, slowly. She is feeling like she will never be able to pull them back up again. She is picturing all the bright red bottoms of all the girls in all the spanking videos she's ever watched. She is feeling like she will be walking around for the rest of her life with her skirt pulled up, and her panties pulled down, and her bright red freshly- spanked bottom on display: on the street, at the grocery store, in the clubs, everywhere, for everyone to see. She pulls down her panties slowly, hanging on to her last shred of dignity for as long as she can.

Her bottom is now bare. One camera is moving freely, ready to watch her whole body, and her breasts, and her face. The other is positioned behind her, to get a continuing close view of her exposed bottom. Dixie takes her by the hand, and pulls her down over her lap. It feels like she's been pushed off a cliff. She clings to the familiar sofa pillow, and presses herself against Dixie's thighs.

She'd been planning to be silent. Her one little piece of defiance. But Dixie's hand comes down on her bare bottom. Her first spank. The years of humiliated hunger come down in that spank, and the years of humiliated exposure ahead of her, and Cherry screams out. She screams in fear and shame and pointless protest, and squirms her ass frantically away from Dixie's hand. She'd been planning to hold still, too. That's not going to happen either. She knows now: she is going to give them a show. She doesn't want to, she hates herself for it, but she can't help it. She is going to wriggle and scream. She is wriggling and screaming now, while her porn star lover spanks her bare bottom on camera. She can't stop it.

Her long fantasies of helplessness and fear and shame, and the immediate reality of her helplessness and fear and shame, are fusing in her head. In her mind's eye she sees herself: an amateur spanking model bent over a porn star's lap, screaming and protesting and wiggling her bare bottom as it turns from pale to pink. Dixie's girl-toy gets spanked for the first time. The image humiliates her further, and she squirms harder to try to escape from it; but instead of providing relief, her squirming cranks the image in her head into sharp, vivid focus. She is soon in a perfect storm, a perpetual motion machine: humiliated at her own humiliation, afraid of her own fear, made helpless by her helplessness. Dixie keeps talking about how bad she is, how dirty, how she got herself into this position, how she deserves to be punished hard on her bare bottom for watching those filthy perverted spanking videos. She believes every word of it.

And yes, the pain. The pain, though, is not what she'd imagined. It is both easier and harder than she'd expected. It's like a roller coaster: terrifying when it comes over the peaks, dizzying when it swoops down through the valleys. But surprisingly, the pain is not the point. The pain, clearly, is the means to an end. The pain is there to make her feel helpless. The pain is there because it isn't a spanking without it. The pain is there to wake her up, to keep her awake and paying attention during every second of her humiliation. The pain is there to drive her humiliation deep into her body. That—the shame—is the point. The pain, she can grit her teeth and endure. The shame, she just has to feel.

She keeps thinking that the shame can't get any harder. And then Dixie does something new, and the volume gets turned up. When she switches from her hand to the hairbrush. When she pulls up Cherry's blouse and pulls down her bra to expose her breasts. When she puts her hands on Cherry's legs to spread her thighs apart. When she starts spanking Cherry again, this time with her breasts bare and her legs spread wide. When she puts her hands down between Cherry's thighs, to spread her cunt lips apart. When the camera comes in close to look at her bright red bottom and her spread-open pussy. When the other camera comes in close to look at her bared breasts, and then her face. She starts to cry, something else she wasn't going to do, and the camera drinks up her tears.

She feels something hard and cool between her legs. Dixie has pulled out a vibrator, from under the cushion or something, and is pressing it against Cherry's clit and turning it on. No, Cherry thinks. No. She can't do this to me. She can't do all this, and then make me come on camera too. Dixie moves the vibrator in little figure eights, the way Cherry had done that time Dixie made her show how she masturbated. It takes no time. In a few seconds, she is coming, sobbing, her legs spread wide, her bright red spanked bottom humping up in the air like a dog in heat.

The shakes keep going through her: she squirms away from them, and at the last moment clutches to hold on to them. Finally, she is finished. She realizes that the room around her is completely silent. She stays in place. She doesn't know what to do next; she's not ready yet to face what her life will be after this. She stays over Dixie's lap with her legs spread, silent except for her hard breathing, and waits for instructions. The director says, "Cut." She waits.

"Jesus, kid. You're a natural."

She twists up to look at Dixie. Dixie is looking at her with a new expression. Respect? No, not quite. Close, though. Dixie is looking at her as if she had value. As if she was worth something. Not respect. But almost.

"Jesus fuck, this is going to be hot. We're going to sell a zillion. We might even win awards. We have to do this again. Hell, I want to do it again right now. And we have to find some other cherries to pop. Have you ever taken it in the ass?"

No.

She can't.

She thinks about lying, saying "Yes" to throw Dixie off the scent. She shakes her head. No. She has never taken it in the ass.

"Good. We'll do that next time. Cherry Bottoms, Dixie's girl-toy, gets fucked in the ass for the first time. See her virgin ass violated as she begs for it to stop and then begs for more. Vince, you can sell that, can't you? Great. Let's set it up. And you... I can't wait to get you home. I have big plans for you."

She sees now what her life will be. She has no power to steer it in another direction. She nods.

Yes. What She's Not Telling Him

Their arrangement is, in theory, completely consensual. Safewords, and limits, and all the usual stuff.

What she's not telling him is that, the moment he orders her in for a punishment, all of that stuff disappears. The moment he tells her that she must be punished—no, even before that, the moment he gets the gleam in his eye that prophecies a punishment—her submission takes over her mind, and her safeword and limits and understanding that she has consented to all this are obliterated. What she's not telling him is that, for her, the game of sadistic master and frightened obedient slavegirl is real, and is becoming more real with each passing week.

In their arrangement, he always initiates the punishments, and she never refuses. It's an arrangement she'd asked for, early on. It's an arrangement he agreed to, with fascination and eagerness: but also reluctantly, and with more than a bit of trepidation. It's an arrangement he thinks is a potential minefield. So he agreed to it only on condition that she absolutely promise to safeword if she needs to, that she promise to tell him immediately if he's being too hard or too cruel.

She promised.

She lied.

For her, the moment her punishment begins, all of her ability to say "No" vanishes.

And that is exactly as she wants it.

Early on in their relationship, after a punishment, he would ask her to give him feedback. Was that too hard? Too fast? Were the things I said too cruel? He would check in after a punishment, or even once or twice during. She soon asked him to please not do that. She says it spoils the mood if he checks in during a punishment; spoils the memory of it if he checks in after. She says he can trust her, that she'll tell him if there's a problem. She tells him that if she doesn't say anything, he can trust that it's all okay with her.

She's lying. She wants it to be too hard. She wants him to do things that are not okay with her. She wants it to be out of her control. He's asked her to tell him if he ever punished her too hard. What she's not telling him is that he has punished her too hard, many times.

So this is what it feels like now.

He gets the gleam in his eye. The spark of the idea. And no matter what she's doing—emptying the dishwasher, reading a magazine, surfing the Internet—her sense of herself as a capable adult in the modern world slips off like a costume. He scolds her, and degrades her, and punishes her... and she feels like a naughty frightened child. Like a disobedient teenager. Like a lowly servant girl on a remote estate. Like a whore in a white slavery brothel.

And when he does sexual things to her, during, or after—when he makes her pose and show off her body, or makes her masturbate for him, or tickles her clit in between strokes of a beating, or simply pushes his cock inside her cunt—she feels like she is being raped. She feels like her body is being forced onto display, like her pleasure is being forced out of her body, like his cock is being forced into her against her will.

He is changing. He used to be a regular kinky guy. He liked to spank girls—who doesn't? He liked to order girls around—big deal. He liked for girls to pretend to be his sex slave—who wouldn't want that? He liked some things a little harder and freakier than most kinky guys, other things a little less hard and freaky. He was well within acceptable limits.

But in response to her complete acceptance of whatever he doles out, he has been changing. He is human, not invulnerable to temptation. People say they wouldn't really want a willing and perfectly compliant sex slave to do their every bidding and never ask for anything of their own. They say that the slave girl/ slave boy thing is a nice fantasy at best; that what they truly want is a partner to share their sexual desires together, someone whose arousal they can enjoy as much as their own. Blah, blah, blah. But who, when presented with a willing and compliant and undemanding slave girl or slave boy, would actually turn it away? Very few, she thinks. Certainly not this one.

And who, when presented with the compliant slave, not as a temporary treat but as a daily reality, a constantly available presence in their everyday lives, would not explore the outer reaches of that compliance, and take further advantage of it with each passing week?

Again: very few, she thinks. Certainly not this one.

So he has been changing. He has been pushing harder, of course: that was to be expected. And he is becoming more cruel. His passion is becoming more brutal; his imagination is becoming more sinister. He used to spank her with the usual array of implements: hairbrushes, paddles, etc.; now, he devotes hours of time and thought to finding and inventing freshly vicious implements to beat her with. He used to order her into poses that were sexy and showed off her body; now, he orders her into poses that are degrading and show off her helplessness. He used to slide his lubed fingers one by one into her asshole after a spanking, to prepare the way for his cock; now, he whips her ass until it's welted and red, and immediately forces his lubed cock into her asshole, and pushes harder when she whimpers and cries.

At first, he was exploring the outer regions of his own desires and fantasies, enjoying the luxury of getting every desire fulfilled immediately, no matter how extreme or trite. Lately, however, it seems as if he's been exploring, not the things that he wants, but the things that she doesn't want: searching for the things that frighten or humiliate her, and taking his pleasure that way. He has made her take pictures of herself, in the poses and costumes he knows she finds most degrading, and has made her post them on the Internet. He has taken her to a sex party, and led her naked on a leash all around the rooms, and then put her on her knees in the center of the main room with a sign around her neck saying "Fuck Any Hole." He has put an ad for her on the Internet personals, offering her services as a blowjob slave, and gone with her to her assignations, making sure only that she is properly on her knees before he closes the door on her.

And it's happening more often. She wasn't sure that would happen—she had been worried that the charm would fade with time, that she would be reduced to bringing him dinner every night and sucking his cock once a week.

But it's not. It's the exact opposite.

He is doing things to keep her in a constant state of humiliation and servitude. He is making her strip naked the moment she walks in the door, and is making her remain naked as long as she is inside. He has ordered her to put clamps on her nipples for five minutes every hour, and has set the alarm on her phone to remind her to do it. He spanks her at least a little bit every morning, before they go to work. He hurts and humiliates her at least a little bit every night, before they go to bed.

He is working to keep her in a state of constant readiness, and constant awareness of her subservience. But these things are working on him as well, keeping him in a constant state of arousal, and a constant awareness of his control over her, and an increasing assumption that this control is his by right.

What's more: He is beginning to forget the few limits she'd set early on. He has forgotten, for instance, that she had said "No" to enemas. When he led her on all fours into the bathroom and began to fill the bag, she was flooded with wordless terror, unable to speak or even shake her head. When he slid the nozzle into her and began to fill her up, she felt something break inside her heart: the one thing she couldn't tolerate, and it was being forced inside her anyway. When he put a plug in her ass and gave her a vibrator and made her masturbate face down on the bathroom floor with her ass full of water, she came harder than she's come in months, weeping, coming apart on the cold tile.

After, he said, "That was amazing. We'll be doing that again soon." The knowledge that she will have to do that again, that it could happen at any time: it fills her with a paralyzed panic, a helplessness that she can never escape from, that she is constantly conscious of, every hour of every day.

Which is exactly what she's been looking for.

She's not quite sure why. She isn't introspective in that way. Maybe she thinks she deserves it. Maybe she thinks this is how the world is supposed to be. Maybe this is just what she gets off on, and it doesn't get her off right unless it's complete.

His punishments are absurdly out of proportion to whatever charges he's trumped up against her. But they are not out of proportion, she thinks, to the real crime: the crime of her deception, the crime of her concealment. She has not quite been able to forget that she engineered all this. In fact, she feels guilty for it, and receives her punishments with greater penitence and acceptance because of it.

But she is trying to forget. She is trying to close that last loophole, to seal off the last exit, to wrap her degradation around her like a blanket and shut out the world.

"There are spots on the wine glasses," he tells her tonight. "Put on the stilettos with the locking ankle straps, and go down to the basement, and get on your hands and knees on the floor, and pull your ass cheeks apart with your hands. I'm going to start by whipping your asshole." She is terrified of him whipping her asshole. Her asshole clenches, and she obeys. She strips, and locks the shoes into place, and descends naked and hobbled into the darkened basement.

Breasts

This is the scenario. Her blouse is pulled down, and her bra, to just under her breasts. It exposes her breasts, and pushes them up.

Her hands are pulled or tied behind her back: partly to immobilize her, but partly just to get her hands out of the way. And to pull her shoulders up and back, displaying her breasts to better advantage. Her head is also being pulled back, by a firm hand pulling her hair: also to get it out of the way, and also to display her breasts more effectively. This is being done, not by her tormenter, but by his friends. His assistants. Or, as she's been calling them in her mind, his henchmen. Like the henchmen of the villains in Batman: faceless, interchangeable, the unthinking hands of their evil master.

Her tormenter is playing with her nipples. He pinches her nipples to make them sore; he then flicks a finger back and forth across one nipple, rapidly, firmly, like a tongue across a clit. Then the other. And then the cycle begins again. The more sore her nipples get, the more sensitive they get to his touch. It is both arousing and intensely frustrating. The sensation is enough to turn her on, and to keep her turned on indefinitely—without being enough to get her off.

Her attention is being forcibly directed to her breasts. So she is not just feeling them. She is thinking about them.

She is thinking about how dirty breasts are.

She is thinking about how, in our male-dominated/ visual- image-obsessed/etc. culture, breasts are primarily not a source of pleasure for women, but an object of desire for men. She is thinking about how, in our etc. culture, they are there to be looked at and admired. She is thinking about how, when they are touched, they are touched not for the pleasure of the woman's breasts, but for the pleasure of the man's hands.

This is the sort of thing that pisses her off in her normal life. And it is the sort of thing that—when her hands are pinned behind her back, when her head is pulled back by her hair, when her blouse and her bra have been pulled down to expose her bare breasts, when her breasts are being toyed with and mauled—sends her into a beautifully vicious circle of excitement and shame.

And she is thinking about how breasts are always on display. She is thinking about how they can never be hidden: they are always in front, leading the way, poking out through T-shirts and sweaters and screaming to the world, "Here I am!" She is thinking about, after all this is over and she walks home in the cooling evening, how conscious she will be of her breasts.

He is turning up the heat now. He has gone from pinching to twisting: sharp, cruel twists with purely vicious intent. He is squeezing her breasts, mauling them, groping them like a frat boy. He is slapping them, hard, and it feels like he's slapping her face.

The pain starts to be too much. Her moans shade up into shrieks and screams, and her tormenter gestures to one of his henchman and has her gagged. Normally he likes to hear her scream; but the point of this particular exercise is that it's about his enjoyment of her breasts, and not about her pleasure or pain. So he has a gag forced into her mouth: so as not to be distracted by the sounds she's making, or by what she might be feeling, or by who she, you know, is. He doesn't want to be distracted from anything that isn't her breasts, and his enjoyment of them.

This has the effect, not only of concentrating his attention onto her breasts, but of concentrating her own. Without the ability to vent, both her pleasure and her pain are amplified. Instead of being let out into the afternoon air, the noises she would be making seem to be channeled down through her throat, and down into her chest, and out into her nipples. Where they are trapped.

He is trying to reduce her: to strip away everything about her that is not a sexual object, everything that is not the sexual body part he's currently getting off on. It's working. In much of her day to day life, she has long, tortured conversations with herself about the nature of identity, and who and what she is. Is she her thoughts? Is she her feelings? Is she her memories? Is she her actions? But at the moment, she has no such doubts. At the moment, she is none of these things. She is her breasts. That is all.

She knows what he's leading up to. He's going to fuck her between her breasts. She doesn't know how, exactly. Will he force her onto her knees? Onto her back? Will he oil her breasts and push them together himself... or have one of his henchmen do it? Will he continue to grope and torture her breasts while he fucks them? Will he put clamps on them, so the torment can continue without further assistance from him? Or will he just fuck them: ignoring her breasts' arousal and suffering, and simply using them as a pleasantly soft, pleasantly firm source of friction?

And what then? Will he give the henchmen their turn, directing them to keep her pinned so they can each jerk off onto her breasts in turn? Will he let her masturbate at the end of it all, with his cum and the cum of his henchmen drying on her breasts as she frantically rubs between her legs, shamed and shameless? Or will he come, and smear his cum over her breasts in one last act of debasement, and then politely request that she cover herself up and leave out the side door?

She doesn't know. He's not there yet. She doubts that he's even close. He's gestured to one of his henchmen, who is bringing him a set of nipple clamps, the ones with the weights you add on one by one. Her breasts can already feel them in advance: pendulous with the weight, the intermittent pain morphing into a constant, increasingly sharp ache. It's going to be a long afternoon.

Footstool

A naked woman is kneeling on a wide footstool or a low table. Her hands are on the floor in front of her; her knees are spread wide. It is not a position of grace or beauty. It is an awkward position. It is a position with one purpose: to place her ass, and her thighs, and her spread-open pussy, on display. To make them available. To place them above her head, and above her heart. Where they belong.

I can't see her face. This is not a problem. This is more than not a problem. This is part of the point.

I can hear her crying. This is also not a problem. This is also part of the point.

She is there willingly. She is crying, she is suffering, but she is holding herself in place. When she jerks her ass away from the blows, she quickly puts herself back into place. She wants to be good. She wants approval and praise for taking her punishment like a good girl; or else she's afraid of the things that will happen to her if she's bad.

She is being beaten. With a hand, in preparation for the hairbrush; with a hairbrush, in preparation for the belt. With the belt.

She is writhing and squirming as she cries. She is squirming in response to the pain. And because she is aroused. And because she knows that the man who's beating her will get off on it.

The man beating her can see her excitement as well as her pain. He continues to beat her. He is happy to see her aroused, but he wants to take her past her arousal, into a place of pure suffering. And into a place of giving in. A place, not just of obedience and compliance, but of a humiliated awareness of her place, and a servile acceptance of it.

Yes, he plans to fuck her. Yes, he wants her pussy wet and open. But when he fucks her, he wants it to be about him. Not about her: not about her desire, or her pleasure. He wants it to be about his cock, sliding into her acquiescent cunt. About his fucked-up need to fuck a woman who's crying and suffering and still holding herself in place. Still putting herself on display. Still making herself available. Still, after everything, placing her ass and her thighs and her spread- open pussy above her head, and above her heart.

Her cries are changing now. The man beating her has moved beyond the careful titration of erotic pain, and has become purely cruel; the beating is steady, and relentless, and has no end in sight. But she is no longer crying in protest. She is crying in sorrow. She is suffering, and she is giving in. She jerks her body away from the hardest blows, and then puts herself back into place, making herself available for more.

The man beating her beats her for a while longer. He drives her sorrow and her defeat deep into her body, whipping it into a lather of humiliation and drinking it in like a cocktail.

And then, belt still in hand, he unzips his fly, and presses his cock against her wet, open, humiliated, acquiescent pussy.

She is still crying.

Yes. He plans to fuck her.

He is fucking her now.

Inspired by a short video found on the Internet.

This Isn't Right

She'd moved in with Uncle Mike when she was sixteen. Her mom had finally died, her dad had been AWOL for years. She barely knew Uncle Mike—when her dad took off, he'd stopped coming around.

It probably wasn't such a good idea: a sixteen-year-old girl moving in with a single man who barely knew her, a man she hasn't even seen in eight years. Child Services didn't love it. But he was Shelley's only living relative who wasn't missing or in jail, what choice did they have. And it turned out, she and Mike got on well. He was a stand-up guy, smart and responsible, not like his brother; she was a smart girl, going places. Everyone figured it'd be okay.

And nobody thought it'd be for more than a couple years. Everyone figured Shelley would get her own place after high school: get a job, or go off to college. But she stayed, and went to college in town. This way, she explained, she only had to work a few hours a week. She could concentrate on her studies. And besides, she and Uncle Mike got along.

This thing between them. It had been there from almost the first. They would sit next to each other on the sofa, watching TV, and the space between them was filled with electrical current. They were more conscious of each other's bodies than if he'd had his arm draped around her or she'd been sitting on his lap. When one of them would get up and then sit back down again, they would sit closer, or farther apart, and both took careful note of which it was, and would try to figure out what it meant.

She knew what she was thinking, but could never be sure what he was. It was the same for him. She would take a step forward—modeling a new dress and asking him what he thought of it, or dressing in a halter and hot pants to work in the garden—and he would flinch away. But then, he would touch her waist to get around her in the kitchen, or hug her a little extra tight before saying goodnight, and she would be the one flinching. She is more frisky, usually, flirting more easily with the idea; he is more reserved, far more uneasy... but in his rare moments of being the one to move, he also seems more serious.

After it happened, she never was sure how he got the idea that what he did would be okay. He must have looked at her browser history on her computer, seen the video site she'd been watching. The site that her friend had sent around as a joke. She had laughed along with everyone else, and then watched it every night since: fascinated, and with growing recognition. Endless versions of the same theme: girls, and their bare bottoms, and hands or hairbrushes or things that were worse. Usually being done by older men. In the ones she kept watching, anyway. In the ones she kept coming back to, again and again. After it happened, when she thought about it, the thought of Mike watching the videos she'd been touching herself to made her shiver. Like she was being stalked; like his dick was following a trail of breadcrumbs to her door.

But it was his car that started it. She'd known not to take it out without permission, but she really thought he'd never find out. Of course she'd dented it. He was really angry. Or at least, he seemed really angry. His car had a dozen dents in it already, but he seemed seriously angry over this one.

"I'm really sorry," she said. "I'll pay to get it fixed."

"That is not the point." They were sitting next to each other on the sofa. She was wearing short gym shorts, and a thin tank top that clung to her chest. The current between their bodies should have been diffused by their argument and their anger. It wasn't. It was turned up.

"That is not the point," he repeated. "The point is that you acted recklessly. The point is that you treated me with disrespect. The point is that you were selfish, and didn't consider my feelings." His voice was rising in pitch. He'd never seemed to care about the car that much.

"Oh, come on," she coaxed. "Don't be mad." She rested her hand on his knee.

And he grabbed her around the wrist, and pulled her body down across his lap. Without hesitating, without apparently thinking, he smacked her hard on her bottom.

And everything changed, as if a hand had wiped the scene.

And the new scene is alien, and overwhelming. The shock, as her body makes contact with his, and as the current running through the empty space between them suddenly shorts out. The rush of adult sexuality and female power, confusingly blended with the feeling of childishness, and frightened, embarrassed, guilty childishness at that. The memory of all the videos she's been watching: all the bare bottoms, all the hands and paddles and everything else raining down in righteous fury, the pinkness or redness or worse, the wriggling, the tears, the bare pussies peering out from under the bare bottoms. The vivid consciousness that this is the thing she had been wanting, and has not been able to think about wanting, and it is happening right now. The drop into helplessness, like she has been dropped into a swimming pool and doesn't know how to swim. The acute, shamed awareness that this is her uncle, and that whatever this is, it isn't right.

She needs time: to adjust, to find her feet. But she isn't getting it. His hand is coming down on her bottom, it's coming down hard, and it isn't stopping. The confusion of feelings is overwhelming her body: she freezes to try to get a grip on it, squirms to try to shake it off. But his hand keeps coming down, and every spank on her bottom wipes out reality anew, and shakes her grip loose.

And it hurts. Somehow, with all the videos she's watched, with all the times she's imagined this with her hand between her legs, it hadn't occurred to her that it would really hurt. Her shorts and her panties are thin, they don't give her much protection, and his hands are big, and strong, and calloused. She cries out. "I'm sorry. Please. I'm so sorry."

He stops, as abruptly as he started.

"This isn't right," he says.

She drops her head, in relief, and disappointment, and terror over what's to come next. Of course this isn't right. But they've stopped now.

Maybe they can pretend it wasn't that bad: just an angry uncle punishing his niece, just a little inappropriately for her age.

"This isn't right," he says again. "I can't do it hard enough like this."

Her shorts are flimsy, with an elastic waist. He pulls them down, and her panties, getting them over her bottom in one quick yank, and then tugging them roughly down past her thighs.

She freezes. The confusion, the shock, the feeling of being a sexual woman, the feeling of being a scared and guilty little girl, the helplessness... the volume on all of it turns up. He looks at her body. She feels him looking.

And he begins again.

His bare hand is now making contact with her bare skin, completing the circuit with each sharp blow. She had been confused before, but now she is crystal clear, and the clarity sharpens with each hard spank of his hand on her naked bottom. Her shorts and her panties are down near her knees, and now he spanks her thighs, too. His rhythm is steady, like a hammer or a piston: but the spanks on her thighs seem harder, and angrier, and they make her squirm hard and cry out in shame. He twines his other hand in her hair, twisting his fingers with each blow on her bottom. He's trying to keep her in place, she thinks; but it feels like a caress, pulsing in her hair and stroking on the back of her neck.

And he starts talking. "Tell me you've been bad." he says. "Tell me you're sorry. Tell me you need me to punish you. Tell me you need me to spank your bare bottom. Say thank you for pulling down your shorts and your panties and spanking you hard on your naked bottom."

She repeats the litany he's giving her, even as he shifts away from talk of punishment and regret, and more and more into talk about her body and her nakedness. She repeats his words, and every sentence makes her ever more conscious of her exposure. Every sentence makes her hyper-conscious of her position: sprawled half-naked across his lap for a spanking, childishly humiliated, and at the same time pornographically sexual. Every sentence feels like her shorts and panties are being pulled down all over again. "I'm so sorry," she says. "Please spank my bare bottom even harder. Please punish my bare bottom until it's bright red. Please keep on spanking my naked bottom and my naked thighs, as hard as you have to to make me learn my lesson. Please punish my naked bottom hard, Uncle Mike."

He stops, again out of nowhere. He rests his hand on her ass, then yanks it back as if he's been burned.

"Go to your room," he said, his voice shaking. "We'll take care of this later."

She clambers to her feet. They both look down at her naked pussy, on clear display for the first time, and she hastily pulls her shorts back up. "I'm so sorry," she whispers. She bolts into her room without a word, and slams the door.

She looks around her disordered teenage room in a panic, and starts to frantically tidy her dressing table. What a mess. She is such a slob. She must be such a pain to live with. After a few minutes, she's cleared off a space. She sets her hairbrush in the middle of the space.

She puts a pillow on the floor, kneels down by the side of her bed, and folds her hands to pray. She hasn't prayed since she was eight. She's not even sure she believes in God anymore. The bed is small, made for a child, really. When she kneels beside it, it only comes up to her waist.

She hears a knock on the door, and hears the door open behind her. Usually he knocks and then waits. She hears him standing behind her. She can almost hear him getting ready to apologize, trying to get out the words he's been rehearsing for the last ten minutes. She reaches back, and pulls her shorts and her panties back down.

She folds her hands in front of her again, and bows her head, and parts her legs, just a little. "I'm so sorry," she says again.

The door to her bedroom closes behind them.

For No Reason

There's always been a reason.

There was the reason for the first time, of course. The big one, the one he first punished her for, the one that could still ruin her life if he told anybody. The one that keeps her coming back, that keeps her from telling anybody what he's been doing.

But even after that, he always gave a reason. A rule broken, a deadline missed, a word spoken without respect. He would call her into his office. He would scowl. He would remind her of the broken rule, the missed deadline, the disrespect. And then—then and only then—he would tell her, "Pull up your skirt, and pull down your panties, and bend over my desk. I have to punish you now."

She has almost been getting used to it. At first, and for a long time, these sessions terrified her, made her squirm with shame. But lately, she has been baring her bottom and bending over his desk, not with fear, but with resignation. Even a hint of boredom. Even the slightest shadow of contempt.

This is not okay with him. He needs her to be afraid. To feel helpless. To feel that all her moorings have been cut, and that she is in his hands. He needs her to feel that the only sure things in her world are him, and his hands, and his desk that is supporting her, and the implements he chooses to use on her.

He knows that what he is about to do is dangerous. Immoral, of course, but also risky: risky not just to his reputation and livelihood, that's a given, but risky also to his mental stability. He knows that he is crossing a bad line, into a bad place. He knows he will never be able to think of himself the same way again. He will never again be able to think of himself as a fair and concerned authority, if somewhat harsh and unconventional. After this, he will have to call himself what he is.

But he needs this, and he is going to do it anyway.

Today, he calls her into his office. He scowls at her. And then he tells her, "Pull up your skirt, and pull down your panties, and bend over my desk."

There's just a hint of a shrug in her shoulders. "Why? What am I being punished for? Sir?" she adds.

He was right about the boredom, apparently, and the contempt. He is doing this just in time. He takes the plunge without hesitation.

"There is no reason," he says. "You're not being punished for anything. Now. Pull up your skirt, and pull down your panties, and bend over my desk."

She stares at him, confused, and wary. "I don't understand."

"What don't you understand? I'm telling you to do something. Do it."

"Why?"

He might as well tell her. It's not like she can do anything about it. He is crossing the line, and he is going to take her with him. "I'm doing this because I can. I'm doing this because I choose to do it. And you are going to do it because I tell you to. Because I have the authority, and you do not. Now. Show me your bare bottom, and bend over."

She is frightened, for the first time in a while. She is off-balance, uncertain of the new rules, not understanding what's happening, or what's going to happen next. So out of habit, and not knowing what else she can do, she obeys. She ducks her head and turns away from him... and she exposes herself to him, hitching up her skirt and pulling her panties down over her bare bottom. For the first time in a little while, she does it with shyness and reluctance, and a fear that seems genuine and fresh. She bends over the desk, and she clutches the other side of it, her hands trembling.

Perfect.

He has her where he wants her, and how he wants her, and he is going to make the most of it. He is going to be cruel. Usually when he spanks her, he is hard, and fast, and punitive. It's brutal, but it's over fast. This time, he wants to take his time. He wants her to feel every blow. He doesn't want her to brace herself against a barrage of blows. He wants every smack of his hand to build on the other, so she feels each of them, and all of them at once.

He smacks his hand down hard onto her white, bare bottom. And then he waits, lets it sink in, before he smacks her again. He spanks her hard, but he spanks her slowly. He lets her squirm, and he watches her squirm, and he waits until the squirming stops before he smacks her again.

And this time, he lets his hand linger, just for a moment, on her trembling bottom, watching the white shading into pink, and feeling the cool skin turning to warm. He's never done that before. He is doing it now.

She is beginning to cry. She hasn't cried for him in a long time. It inflames him. He lets himself go harder, the cruelty of the slow beating cascading into the cruelty of a relentless one. And he lets himself go further, the light lingering of his hand after a blow shading into a caress. And then into a grope.

He sees her naked pussy peeping out from between the bright pink cheeks of her bottom. Taunting him. Beckoning him. He has never done anything about it before. Nothing, except wait until she left his office and shut the door to leave him in privacy. Nothing, except call her back into his office, week after week, to get another glimpse.

He's gone this far. He might as well. It's not like she can do anything about it. He is crossing the line, and he is taking her with him.

He silently unzips his trousers, and pulls out his cock. He comes up closer behind her, and puts his hand on her pink, warm, inviting bottom. He squeezes, a long, lascivious grope. "Open your legs," he tells her.

She is still crying. She is frightened, she is confused, she is ashamed. She is clinging to his desk like it's the one sure thing in the world. And slowly, like a pair of iron gates leading to a bright mansion on a hill, she opens her legs.

He touches her pussy with one finger. She sobs harder, and the sound is like a hand pulling him in. Across the line. Down. He fingers her for a moment, drinking in the sight from this side of the line for the last time: her helpless body, her disarranged clothing, her pink pussy, her exposed bottom, her cheeks still pink and warm from being beaten for no reason, her body shaking with fear and confusion and uncontrollable tears.

It draws him in. He forces his cock inside her, hard, and falls.

Changing the Scene

He has been incredibly good throughout all of this.

He is about to stop being good.

He is about to change the scene.

When she first came to him, he had been good. He figured out almost immediately what she wanted, but he restrained his usual sarcastic impatience, and gently guided her to her confession. With some self-interest, to be sure; but also with a genuine, if grudging, concern.

When she finally admitted what she wanted him to do to her, he wanted to comply immediately: to shove her over his desk, to shove her skirt up and her panties down, to punish her bare bottom until she cried. He has known her for years—the last few of those years spent trying to set aside the sordid thoughts he had about her, knowing it was unforgivable for a teacher to even think of a student that way. And now that she was offering herself, now that it was no longer morally repugnant to take advantage of her, he wanted to do it at once, to cruelly violate the young, vulnerable flesh that was being offered him on a silver platter. But he was good, and while he had to bite his tongue many times, he talked her through her circumstances—the too-early marriage, the well-meaning dolt of a husband, the recent separation— to help her make sure she wasn't acting rashly, and was making the right decision in coming to him.

And when she looked at him tearfully after their long conversation and said, "Can we do it now, please?" he wanted nothing more than to grab her by the ear, and drag her over to his desk, and show her exactly what it was she was asking for, and make her sorry she had ever asked.

But he was good. He talked her through the negotiation, introduced her to limits and safewords and whatnot. And when they were done talking, he summoned all his self-control, and said, "You should really think about this. If you still want this a few days from now, then we'll proceed. Are you free a week from today?"

And then, when she came back a week later, exactly on time, he was very good indeed.

He is used to unleashing himself. His wife has been receiving his most vicious attentions with transcendent joy for some years now, and he has become unused to holding back. But he knows this girl had never done this before. So he takes it slow. He is firm, as he knows she wants him to be; but he is careful, titrating out the pain and the shame with the hand of a chemist.

It is important to her that this should be about punishment; that he should be pitiless but fair; that he should be correcting her, and inspiring her to do better. So he counts out her offenses, and marks them on a chalkboard in her line of sight, and erases the marks as he proceeds through her punishments. Offenses against the world, and against him. Her offenses against him are few, but he counts them for much more.

It is important to her that she be exposed. But she is overcome with sudden shyness when he instructs her to do it, to lift her skirt and lower her undergarments. He generally likes women to expose themselves for him—it makes him feel desired, and powerful—but it soon becomes clear that she can't. So he does it for her. He only gives her the barest hint of a withering look, and two marks for her disobedience in the "offenses against me" column. One for her skirt, and one for her panties.

It is important to her that this be a little bit hard. Not too hard, but a little. She wants him to be a little forceful, to make her a little afraid, to make her take a little more than she thinks she wants. So he holds his black rage tightly in check. He limits himself to his hand, and to a wooden ruler at the very end. Her bottom turns bright pink, and then bright red; but it should fade soon, with no bruises. And he keeps his tongue in check: keeping his language harsh but not brutal, his tone biting but not vicious. She has tears in her eyes when he is done, but her pussy is wet, and she seems essentially fine.

And he lets her come. In fact, he orders her to come, in the exact way she most likes to come. He had asked her about this the week before, and he now instructs her to do it: to stay bent over, and to open her legs, and to use the device that she likes to use on herself, the one he told her to bring. He fondles her sore bum while she does it: keeping her punishment vividly in her consciousness, while not distracting her from the business at hand. She tightens up when she goes over the top, and then she collapses, her long unruly hair tumbling about her, her face glowing as pink as her bottom. She sighs a sigh of deep relief and satisfaction.

"I think I'm done," she says.

His black rage slips the leash.

He is about to stop being good.

He is about to change the scene.

He stands back and surveys her. "You think we're done. Do you."

His voice has changed. His voice brims over with dismissal and contempt, a sneer in audible form. It's the voice he used to use in the classroom: the one that made her tremble for seven years, the one that made her wet between her legs for the last three of those years. It's the voice that says, "Your imperfection, predictable though it is, is a cruel disappointment." It's the voice that makes her self-possession crumble: the voice that makes her desperate to please, and unbearably ashamed at not doing so. Her loose, casual sprawl freezes on his desk.

He continues, the temperature in his voice dropping with every sentence, and the poison in it rising. "You think you can come in here, and flaunt your bare bottom at me, and entice me into spanking you for your own pleasure, and spread your legs in front of me while you whack yourself off... and then walk out the door, with merely a 'Thank you.' No, actually, come to think of it. Not with a 'Thank You.' 'I think I'm done.' Charming. Excellent manners. Very thoughtful."

He pries her fingers from the death-grip they have on the far side of the desk, and pins her wrists behind her back. She gasps, taken aback at his surprising strength and the sudden shift in the wind, and he uses her moment of imbalance to seize his opportunity. He has a length of rope in his desk drawer. Her wrists are bound behind her back before she knows it.

She panics. He is angrier than she has seen him in years, and there is nothing and no-one here to stop his anger from breaking over her. She is essentially helpless. She could probably stand up, if he weren't standing right behind her with his hips pushing angrily between her thighs. If he stepped away, she might even make it to the door. But it is a long, winding staircase up out of his cellar. With her hands bound behind her back, she would never make it. He would overtake her in seconds.

"I'll scream," she says.

"Yes," he drawls. "I expect so."

He unlocks the wall cabinet and selects an implement. The crop, he decides. Cruel, but not brutal. Something he doesn't have to hold back with. Something he can use for as long as he needs to. He paces in front of her, tapping it lightly in his hand.

"Now," he says. "Tell me we're done. Tell me we're done, and walk out that door." He gestures to the door with the crop. "And we will be done for good. Or tell me you're sorry, and we can complete this."

She is suddenly ashamed. His voice makes her feel fifteen again: small, trying to be bigger, acutely conscious of her imperfections, deathly afraid of his contempt. She doesn't know if she'll ever again find someone to do these things to her. And she feels genuinely bad for her selfishness. The decision is easier than she would have thought; it makes itself in her mind in a moment, and she speaks before it can change.

"I'm very sorry, sir."

The honorific slips in naturally, as if they had never left school. "Fine," he replies. "That's a start."

He goes to the chalkboard and makes several marks, on the "offenses against me" side. She blanches. The memory is still vivid of what even one mark on that side of the board has cost her. He snarls at her again. "Do you think that's fair, young lady? Does that meet with your approval? Is that to your liking?"

She nods meekly. He shuts his mouth and grips the riding crop: her mind makes itself up again, and again she speaks before she can stop it. "Actually, sir—it's not fair."

Before his rage can explode, she races on. "You haven't given me enough. I messed up badly. I need to show you how sorry I am. I think you may need to give me some more marks." She shuts her eyes tight. "Please, sir. Whatever you were planning to give me—please give me more."

He looks at her suspiciously. He can't decide if she's gaming him to get more smacks out of him. He looks at her face, terrified at what she's just said, and realizes she's sincere. She takes this business of learning lessons seriously. She always did. He makes five more curt marks on the board, and moves into place behind her.

Her bottom has the gently blended pink tinge of a peach. A vicious slash rises up out of it with the first lash of the crop. She screams. As promised. His rage had been cooling a bit, but her scream stirs it up again.

His darkest rages are rarely chaotic. They are all about control: tight, vicious control, laced with sarcasm and an intense desire to hurt as deeply as possible. He lays the lashes in neat, parallel lines across her bottom. He does it in a rhythm, letting each lash blossom onto her skin and into her brain, letting the full rise of the pain and the ebb of the afterburn flow through her body, before he strikes again. He lays the hard stripes all the way down her bottom, and then down the backs of her thighs.

He does it again, filling in the spaces between the marks.

And then again. Twice as many this time. Filling in the spaces between the old marks and the new.

Her screams have fused together into a long animal wail, much the way her welts are fusing into one bright red inflammation. Much the way his arousal has fused into his rage. He lashes her across the old marks now, and his cock rises as the welts rise up higher. He is being careful now to place the blows at random, so she can't predict where they will land next, so each stroke lands like it's coming out of nowhere. Her wailing and her tears run through his veins like Viagra.

He stops. He wipes one mark off the board.

And he begins to rebuke her again, in that cutting voice that makes her want to hide in a closet and cry until she dies; a voice that makes her wish he'd start whipping her again, if only he'd stop saying these things.

"You think this is all about you. You think this is all about your naughty little fantasies of getting spanked on your bottom. You think you can dangle yourself in front of me, and get me to give you what you want, and then walk off without a care. You think you're special, like you're the only girl in England who likes to get her bum smacked. Like there aren't a thousand other girls hungry for the same bloody thing. Like your need to get it trumps everything. You are beyond selfish."

He unbuttons his trousers and takes out his cock. "I have wanted to fuck you for years. I am going to fuck you now. This is what I want. I am going to take it from you. Get ready."

He forces himself hard into her cunt. It takes no effort: she is sobbing, but she is also sopping wet. He almost wishes she wasn't; he wants it to be hard for her, wants to hurt her inside as well as out. But it also makes him feel cruel in a different way, a way he likes better. He likes that he can whip her viciously, and berate her cruelly, and make her pussy wet doing it. It makes him feel desired, and powerful. He draws it out as long as he can, jabbing, thrusting in deep, hoping to make her sore, hoping to make her wish he'd stop so he can keep going anyway. She grimaces—maybe from the marks still blooming on her ass, maybe from his cock forcing itself inside her—and he takes a handful of her tangled hair, and twists it cruelly, and comes.

She is still crying. The crop is on the desk by his hand. He picks it up, and knocks over the chalkboard. "I'd wipe all the marks off," he says, "but I don't feel like moving just now. I'll do it in a bit. Consider them gone."

He unties her hands, and she drops to her knees and embraces him around his waist. "I'm really sorry," she says, still sniffling. "I didn't mean to hurt your feelings. I really wanted you to fuck me. I was just feeling good, and I was thoughtless. I'm sorry."

Not many people in his life have said they didn't mean to hurt him. His wife, and their lover. His best friend. His oldest friend, before things went so wrong. The last tatters of his rage and hurt dissipate. He kneels down next to her, and rests his hand on her bottom, lightly, gingerly. He knows better than to apologize. "Checking," he says. "Was that too much?"

She shakes her head, laughing, wiping her wet face with the back of her hand. "Fuck, no. That was... I mean, it was.... Okay, not so much what I expected. But no. Not too much. Just right."

When he first met his wife, when they spent that first bizarre night together, she said that sex with him was like being hit by an intelligent hurricane: it rearranged all the furniture, and she had to figure out where everything was and how it all fit together now that he was here. He can see that he has already begun rearranging his own furniture, just a bit, to make room for this young woman. Not for long, probably: she is only twenty-two, new to the world in many ways. She'll discover soon that he is far from the only person who will do these things to her; that England is full of lovely young men who will happily wallop her bottom as hard as she likes. But for now, she is here is in his arms: beautiful, brilliant, needing attention, apparently wanting the rather distinctive attentions that he has to give. She seems to be one of those rare people who sees him as he is, and likes him anyway. He hopes the feeling outlasts this affair. There are not many people in his life whom he likes. He seems to like her.

He sees that she is still wet down there. "Would you like to come again?" he asks, as if he's offering her a cocktail.

She nods, and reaches a tentative hand towards her cunt. "May I?"

He moves her hand aside, and reaches between her legs. "Allow me."

UNICORNS AND RAINBOWS

The Unicorn and the Rainbow

Frank the unicorn walked into the bar. Midnight, pissing rain, and the grime on the neon-garish windows streaked down the glass like a whore's mascara. The unicorn staggered across the floor and slammed his hoof on the bar. "Jack. Double shot."

The bartender eyed him. Sizing up how drunk he was already, how much of a pain in the ass it would be to 86 him, whether or not he gave a damn. He shrugged, and poured the double shot. In a sop to his not-quite-dead sense of responsibility, he plonked a glass of water next to it. The unicorn glared at the water like it had been dredged from the toilet. "What. The fuck. Is that."

A voice shimmered from the end of the bar. "Rough night?"

The unicorn glared in the direction of the voice. A rainbow was draped on a barstool, his hot colors crossed elegantly over his cool ones at the bottom, all seven of his tendrils waving gracefully, if a bit unsteadily, at the top.

The unicorn snorted. "What the fuck business is it of yours how rough a night I'm having?"

"I could make it my business. And I like it rough."

The rainbow sidled over to the unicorn and ordered another vodka. "So. How old was she? Twelve? Thirteen? Who'd she throw you over for?"

The unicorn's ivory face turned dead white. "How... how did you..."

The rainbow shrugged. "Oh, please. It's all over your face. So who was it? A boy band? A sitcom star? Some twerp from American Idol? It

89

must have been bad. You look like you've been in every bar from here to Middle Earth."

An ugly flush of rage flashed into the unicorn's face, and for a second, the rainbow thought he might get punched in the gut. Then the unicorn collapsed onto the bar. A single, silvery tear trickled down his face.

"That actor. The one in the vampire movies. Robert something. She—she tore down all my posters. Scraped my stickers off her desk. She even threw out her trapper keeper. Now this moody undead wanna-be is all over her bedroom, and it's like I never existed."

The rainbow patted him on the shoulder. "That's not so bad, pal. There's dignity in a vampire. You could do worse. Hey, my last one threw me over for Justin Bieber."

The unicorn flinched. "What do you mean—your last one?"

"Sweetie," the rainbow chuckled grimly, "I've been dropped for every teen idol since 1967. David Cassidy, Corey Feldman, Hanson... hell, I even got dumped for Ringo Starr. And that was *after* the Beatles broke up. Please. Don't tell me this is your first."

The rainbow glanced at the unicorn's stricken face. "Oh. Fuck. If I'd known... Look, pal. You gotta learn to take these things lightly. That's how the game is played. They love you like a mental patient, they can't get enough of you, you're their entire world... and right when they're hitting puberty and it's starting to get interesting, they drop you like a hot rock, for whatever non-threatening boy the teen idol machinery is pumping out this week. That's how it goes. Did you really think it was going to last? Would you even want that?" The rainbow shuddered. "Imagine a forty-seven year old woman who's into unicorns. I've been down that road. Believe me, you're better off. Ride the ride, get off when it ends, have a drink or twelve, get back in line and strap yourself in again. It's not a bad life. And there are... consolations."

The rainbow downed his drink. "Come on. Back alley. I said I liked it rough. You're having a bad night? Take it out on me. Pretend I'm Ashley or Brianna or whatever the fuck her name was. Smack me around; call me a treacherous whore; fuck me six ways from Sunday like you could never fuck her. It'll make you feel better. Trust me."

A few beads of purple sweat rose up on the rainbow's forehead as he spoke, putting the lie to his casual tone, and a faint smell of lavender filtered into the dank room. The unicorn glowered... and then grabbed the rainbow by his red tendril, and dragged him out the side door.

The alley stank of cum, and of cheap sushi from the buffet at the strip club next door: a deep-grained stench the rain had barely made a dent in. The rainbow was sweating hard now, the lavender scent rising out of his body like steam from a manhole cover, and the smell of lavender and sushi and cum mingled into a harsh, strange perfume: discordant, yet heady, even intoxicating. The unicorn, intoxicated already, was overcome: his knees buckled, and the rainbow seized his advantage. He lashed a tendril around the unicorn's cock, and squeezed. The unicorn flinched in shock, then smacked the rainbow hard, his hoof lashing a deep cut into his face. A gush of indigo blood leaked into the rainbow's eyes. He grimaced. "Yes. Harder."

The unicorn struck again, and again, as the rainbow tightened his grip on his cock and began stroking in earnest. "Yes," the rainbow purred. "That's it. Beat me down. Spank me like a bad, bad donkey." The rainbow spread his tendrils out like an octopus, stretching the tips to tickle the unicorn's balls, and clamp onto his nipples, and twine into his silvery mane, and sneak into his asshole. The unicorn was overwhelmed with sensation: his blows against the rainbow's bloody face became staggered and irregular, like a heartbeat in cardiac arrest, and his cock throbbed like a bruise.

The rainbow suddenly twisted around. He bent sharply at the waist, and spread his green and blue tendrils apart, wrapping them to form a tight hole around the unicorn's cock. "She'd never let you fuck her, would she? Well, fuck me now. Fuck me hard. Fuck all that pain and rage out of you. Bitch didn't want you? Bitch didn't deserve you. Bitch wouldn't know what to do with you." The unicorn screamed like a slaughterhouse, and came, spewing a fountain of mercury into the rainbow's fuckhole and across the alley. He shuddered, and passed out, collapsing in a heap beside the garbage cans.

The rainbow took a quick glance to make sure the unicorn was still breathing, and that he was really out. Then he snatched up the unicorn's satchel and rummaged through it. A few crumbs of pink cupcake. A battered copy of "Ender's Shadow" by Orson Scott Card. A wallet. Bingo. The rainbow rifled through it. A ten, a few ones. A lottery ticket. A crumpled photo of a pretty blonde girl in a pink unicorn sweatshirt, torn down the center through the girl's face, then taped back together with Scotch tape. The rainbow looked at the unicorn, passed out next to the trash cans, the tracks of his tears still silvery on his pale, moonlit face. He rolled his eyes, and put the wallet back in the satchel.

"It's okay, pal," he said. "This one's on me."

RELIGION

Christian Domestic Discipline

She sometimes forgets that this was her idea.

She's getting confused about this, and she forgets that she's the one who talked him into it. She forgets that she's the one who found the Website, with the handbook and the Bible quotes and the stories: all that stuff about how God wants husbands to decide and wives to obey, how it was God's will for a husband to physically chastise his wife, how it restored the natural order of a marriage for a husband to spank his wife when she misbehaves. She forgets how intriguing she found it: like an adventure in marriage, an exciting secret with God's blessing. She forgets how eager she was to show him the stories: the devotion of the rituals, the constant cycles of defiance and penitence, the loving attention to the physical details of implements and undergarments and bare bottoms being revealed. All by command of the inerrant word of God.

His reaction to it—now that, she remembers. He was shocked: but not the way she'd expected. Not at the ideas or the stories. He was shocked that it was her presenting them. He kept asking her, "Don't you know?" "Don't you know what people think of this stuff?" "Don't you know that this stuff is sick?" When she showed him the stories, it was like he'd been reminded of an unsettling dream he'd been trying to forget. And when she showed him the handbook, with its extensive explanations of why this sort of relationship was not only accepted by God but sanctioned and blessed by Him, he looked both relieved and ashamed, like he'd been given permission to do something he knew was sinful and terrible.

But she forgets that it was her idea. She forgets how hard she pleaded with him to at least try it; how happy she was when he cautiously agreed; how excited she was the first time he told her that she'd been bad and he was going to do it right then and there.

She forgets because it's hard. It hurts, and it's hard.

Parts of it are okay. That's part of why she's confused. Parts of it are a lot like how she imagined when she first found the website. The shy excitement when she pulls down her panties; the thrill of fear when she refuses and he pulls them down for her; the rush of helplessness when he takes her over his knee; the struggle for power; the revelatory joy of giving in; the softness and openness and sense of rightness with God and the world when it's over and her husband has put her in her place.

But when the hard blows are landing on her bare bottom, it hurts. Sometimes it hurts too much. Sometimes it hurts more than she can take... and it doesn't matter, he's in control, she has to take it anyway. The literature says that he doesn't need her consent for this; the law may disagree, it says, but God has given the husband the right to discipline his wife as he sees fit. She didn't take that seriously at first. Now, when she's writhing and crying and begging for mercy that isn't coming, she knows exactly what it means.

She's read the literature. She knows that it has to really hurt for it to work, that it has to hurt too much. She knows that hurting too much is what takes a disobedient wife from protest to panic, and from panic to surrender and remorse and obedience. But when it's hurting too hard, and she's struggling and crying and begging him to stop... then she doesn't know how this started, or where it's going, or anything at all except panic and pain. The panic overwhelms her, and the surrender seems a million miles away. She tries not to struggle—she knows struggling will just get her punished harder—but her reflexes kick in, and she fights it, outraged, terrified, desperate. When he pulls down her panties and punishes her hard, it feels like the hand of God is driving into her bare bottom. And she has no more power to stop it than she does to stop God.

So she's confused. Her feelings about it are all mixed up, and she forgets that she set this into motion.

Plus she forgets because it's changing.

At first, it was just like in the stories she'd read. He'd scold her and make her pull down her panties, or if she was sulky and defiant he'd pull them down for her. He'd spank her with his hand, or with her hairbrush if she'd been especially naughty. He'd make her say out loud what a bad girl she was, how sorry she was for disobeying him. And then he'd make love to her. It was a little difficult sometimes, but it was naughty and fun and actually pretty close to what she'd hoped for. An exciting secret that the two of them shared with God.

But lately, it's been harder. He's using all these different things—the instruments of God, he calls them—to punish her. She's lucky now if she just gets the hairbrush. If she makes a mistake in the kitchen, now she gets the metal spatula. If she makes a mistake in the yard or the garden, now he makes her cut him a switch. If she spends too much time on the phone or the computer, he takes the phone wire, and folds it up several times in his hand, and whips her with that. And if she's been particularly bad—or if he's in a particularly wrathful mood—he gives her the belt. He seems to have special feelings about the belt. It's starting to make her squirm just to see him wearing it. He wears it every day.

And lately, he's been doing these... things. Things that aren't in any of the stories she's read. He's been making her get into positions—awkward positions, humiliating positions, positions that make her feel like a whore or an animal—while he punishes her. He's been making her say things while he punishes her: not just saying she's sorry and begging forgiveness, but dirty things, things she'd never heard of until he made her say them, things that make her want to crawl in a hole just to think about. He's been making her get into positions, and then he's been making her use her fingers to spread herself open, down there, exposing her privates for him to look at, while he punishes her.

He says it's all part of the punishment. He says it has to be hard on her: if it's not hard, it's not punishment. He says he's trying to punish, not only her body, but her soul. He says it's not enough to make her suffer: he has to make her feel ashamed.

And then he makes love to her.

The literature says that marital relations will often follow a punishment. It assures her that this doesn't mean anything sick, that it simply shows the husband's natural eagerness to be intimate with his wife once his rightful authority has been restored and their relationship has been returned to God's vision for marriage. But she's starting to wonder. He never made love to her like this before they started the discipline. He whips her and humiliates her, and he pushes himself into her with passion and fury.

So she's confused.

The pain and the shame are hard. And they're getting harder. They make her feel frightened, and small. She jumps at the sound of his voice now: desperate to please him, terrified that she's let him down. She used to feel easy and relaxed with him; now she feels like every day of their marriage is Judgment Day.

And yet, it also makes her feel... she doesn't have a word for it. Not a nice word, not a word she could say when he isn't whipping her bare bottom and telling her to say it. But she feels that way all the time now. Not just when they're making love. When she cooks with the metal spatula; when she brushes her hair; when they go over the bills together. She thinks about his wrathful hand coming down on her bare bottom, and the crude, shameful things he makes her say, and her bottom glowing and tingling when her punishment is over, and his body looming over her as he spreads her apart and forces himself into her. It makes her feel... her mind flinches away from the words for how it feels, but it lingers on the feeling itself.

And she's not even sure anymore which parts she likes and which she doesn't. The pain is hard: but after a while it makes her feel rapturous too, the way the martyrs must have felt when they mortified their flesh for God. The shame is hard: but it also makes her feel wide open, like her walls have come tumbling down and she's completely vulnerable and available. The pain and the shame are starting to feel like more than a means to an end. They're starting to feel like the point. When she's being chastised, the pain and the shame are how she feels the hand and the voice of God in her husband's hand and voice.

She doesn't know if she should feel this way. She's confused. But if he's confused, he's not showing any signs of it.

He is strict and unyielding, just like the literature says he should be. He says that if he lets her decide when she should be punished, and how, then he'd be letting her have control of the marriage, and that's not what God wants. He never shirks responsibility, never throws it in her face that she's the one who started this. He took the reins with some trepidation at first; but he is gripping them more firmly every day, and is showing no signs of letting go.

But she's confused. So she lets him keep deciding. She is confused and weak, the way God created women; and he is strong and resolute, the way God created men. And she knows how she feels when she's melting in his arms after he's punished her and made love to her. She's confused... so she's going to keep letting him guide her and decide for her. She's going to keep putting herself into his hands, and thus into God's.

She's thinking about all this as she cooks Sunday breakfast. He walks into the kitchen. "Hurry up," he insists. "We don't want to be late for church." She jumps at the sound of his voice, and scratches the pan with the metal spatula.

Inspired by the Christian Domestic Discipline website and fiction.

Penitence as a Perpetual Motion Machine

"I'm here to see Sister Catherine."

"Yes. It's nice to see you again, Mary. Please have a seat. Catherine has just finished up with another—visitor. Why don't we take care of business now. She'll be with you in a moment."

Mary Elizabeth nods. She hands the woman behind the desk four hundred dollars in cash, and sits, keeping her coat on and her purse clutched in her lap. She tries not to look at the lobby: the garish red and black decor, the velveteen curtains tied back with steel chains, the worn spot on the black leather sofa. It makes it harder for her to think of this the way she needs to think of it. She sits, and stares at her knuckles gripping the handle of her purse, and waits.

"Mary Elizabeth. Please come in."

Catherine has stepped into the lobby. She is dressed, as always for their meetings, in a modified modern habit: the knee-length gray dress, the heavy hose and sensible shoes, the small, unimposing wimple. She has carefully wiped all traces of makeup from her face.

She takes Mary Elizabeth by the hand, and leads her to the now-familiar room, the one fitted up like a schoolroom. An office or rectory would have been better, but this was the closest they had.

"Sit down, Mary. We have to have a difficult conversation."

Mary Elizabeth—formerly Sister Mary Elizabeth—left the convent a little over two years ago. She left, more in need of penance than when she arrived. She left, unwilling to let the Church ever tell her a blessed thing about right and wrong again. She left, desperately needing

100

somebody to tell her that she has done wrong, and to administer justice for it. So she comes here.

At Sister Catherine's gesture, she sets down her purse and takes off her navy blue coat. She is dressed, as always for their meetings, in a Catholic schoolgirl uniform. A real one, ordered from one of her own convent's suppliers, the ones for the older girls fit her awkwardly but adequately. She sits, her hands behind her back, shaking. Knowing, in a general way, what is about to come, and being terrified of it anyway. Not knowing, specifically, what is to come, and being more terrified of that. Sister Catherine begins.

"So, Mary. I think you know what we're here about. The incident at school yesterday. One of the girls was badly hurt. I know that you weren't one of the main girls involved, but I know you were there, and you didn't stop it, or tell any of the sisters or fathers about it. This is a serious matter. Two other girls have been expelled, they may even be arrested. But you have a good record, and you weren't as deeply involved, so I have persuaded Father Dominic to let you stay on, with a less severe sentence. I have told him that I would handle your penance.

"We will start simply. Bend over this desk. Raise your skirt, and lower your drawers."

All of this part is scripted. All of this part—the lecture, the position, the implement— is the same every time. The content of the lecture isn't perfect, but it's the closest she could come to what really happened without saying too much. It took Mary some time to find a... professional... who was willing to work with a script, even a short one. But Sister Catherine seems to have some genuine affinity for the script. She says the lines with passion and intensity; she wields the implement with grim determination. And Sister Catherine seems also to appreciate the free hand that she has with Mary once the scripted part is completed. Sometimes, she seems to appreciate it rather too much. Mary always pays for two hours: the scripted part is usually over in twenty minutes. Sister Catherine never has trouble filling the rest of the time.

Mary complies at once with the instructions. She is praying that it won't be too hard. But she is also, deep in her mind, praying that it will be. She is thanking God that she was caught. She is wracked with guilt over her crime, and the guilt is stronger than the fear. She immediately bends over the desk and raises her skirt to her waist. She lowers her underwear, more slowly, reluctantly: still, after all these times, feeling the shame rise up in her body with the lowering of the fabric and the revelation of her naked flesh. When her underwear has finally been lowered, she stretches across the desk and clutches the edge... praying that the punishment will be hard, viciously hard, unbearably hard, so her guilt will be cleansed, and she won't have to feel the way she feels.

The first stroke of the cane lands on her bared bottom like the fires of Judgment. Mary screams. She always thinks she'll be ready for this, and she never, ever is. Her scream seems to inspire Sister Catherine to greater wrath, and the next blow lands harder.

She has asked Sister Catherine never to tell her how many lashes she's going to get. If she knows how many, she knows she'll hang to the last one like a life raft. She doesn't want to do that. She needs to drown. She needs the pain to feel like it might never end. Sister Catherine is happy to oblige. She is happy to let the rising pitch of Mary's screams be a signal, not that she should slow down, but that she should turn up the volume.

It works. The guilt begins, ever so slightly, to break up inside her. The first lash on her naked backside breaks off a piece of her guilt, like a chunk of ice breaking off a glacier; the lashes that follow crush that chunk into smaller and smaller pieces: pieces that are small enough to melt and spill out of her body.

It works. But there's an obstacle: an obstacle that arises every time she lowers her panties to receive Sister Catherine's judgment. An obstacle she should have expected, given her history, but one that she nevertheless doesn't how to handle.

The obstacle is that, on the days before she meets with Sister Catherine, she is filled with a gruesome excitement. She remembers or imagines the lash of Catherine's cane; she remembers or imagines her helplessness and shame, her position bent over the desk with her backside exposed, the other—things—that Sister Catherine has made her do... and she touches herself. She imagines the things she's afraid Sister Catherine might make her do next time... and she touches herself. She touches herself, until she finds release. On the rare occasions that Sister Catherine has forced her to masturbate as part of her penance, she has obeyed, with a familiarity and a lack of reticence that she knows must be a dead giveaway.

All of which means that now, she has something new to feel guilty about.

So even as her old guilt is being demolished by Sister Catherine's blistering justice, new guilt is building up behind it. And so she has to keep coming back. For weeks, months. Perhaps for years. She doesn't know yet where this is going, or how it will end.

Penitence as planned obsolescence. Penitence as a fraudulent physician who makes his patients sick so he can keep treating them. Penitence as a perpetual motion machine.

The storm finally breaks. Sister Catherine has beaten Mary Elizabeth through her screams, through her hysteria, through her frantic clawing and pounding on the desk. She has beaten Mary Elizabeth until hellish red welts rose up out of her backside, and has then echoed those marks on the backs of her thighs, and has then repeated the theme of merciless justice, with variations, back on her backside again.

But she seems to have received an invisible signal, and has finally set down the cane, and is standing behind Mary, considering. Mary tries to catch her breath, clutching the far side of the desk, feeling the criss-cross of welts rising up out of her flesh like an alphabet of scarlet letters, advertising her shame to the world. She tries to catch her breath, tries to feel relief at the brief respite. She tries not to feel dread. She tries not to feel the other things she feels when she thinks about this. The scripted part, the familiar part, is over. The unknown part is coming up.

"And now," Sister Catherine says, "we will move on."

Her voice has changed. The solemn voice of disappointment and censure is gone, and has become gleefully sinister. The voice of the Wicked Witch crowing over her beautiful wickedness. The voice that speaks, not of justice, but of malice. The voice that Mary replays in her head when she touches herself.

Mary is beginning to think that Sister Catherine has figured out the truth. Or has figured out something that's close to the truth. The standard punishments have been growing more severe; the improvised punishments have been growing more... imaginative. In recent months, Mary has had to lie on her back with her legs parted, and say ten Hail Marys while Sister Catherine whipped her between her legs. She has had to lie face down on the floor and lick Sister Catherine's shoes, with her skirt still raised and her drawers removed and her legs opened wide, while Sister Catherine flicked her between the cheeks of her backside with something slim and vicious, and told her this was where bad girls had to be punished. She has had to put her body into positions of in-dignity and gross obscenity, and has then had to beg Sister Catherine to chastise her again in each new position. She has had to drink two quarts of water, and then let Sister Catherine cane her again until she wet herself. She has had to administer fellatio to this... thing, an object shaped like a phallus but with an image of Christ on the cross molded on the surface in relief. She had to flick the tip of her tongue rapidly up and down Christ's body, and tell him how sorry she was for being wicked and adding to his suffering, and then thrust the profane object deep down her throat... while Sister Catherine traced the welts on her backside with a sharp fingernail, and murmured a stream of obscenities into her ear.

She has allowed all of it to happen.

Because she knows what she did.

She never did any of it herself. But she knew. She had even, on a few occasions, been in the room when the incidents began. And been ordered out of the room before they were completed. Twice, she had been ordered to assist: to pin down a pair of struggling hands, or hold her hand over a screaming mouth, while the incidents happened from behind. Those were two of the times that she was asked to leave the room: times that she knew the incidents were going to continue, and were going to get worse, after she left.

She had known. She had even seen it, some of it. And she hadn't tried to stop it, or told anybody.

So this seems like justice.

"Stay in place," Sister Catherine says. "We're going to move forward now."

Mary hears stirring behind her. She tries not to imagine what is happening, what is being prepared for her. Then she feels it. Something hard, and cold, and slippery, being pressed against the opening between her legs.

Mary freezes.

Over the weeks and months, Sister Catherine has done unspeakable things to her. She has trespassed almost every law of human decency that Mary could imagine, and many that Mary had never known existed. But she has always stayed within the boundaries of the house rules, and of the law. Mary can't find her voice, but she shakes her head fiercely. No. Not this. Sister Catherine stops, and speaks.

"Do you think this is unfair?" she sneers. "Really? Given your crimes, given the things that you did—and the things that you failed to do—do you really and truly consider this an unfair punishment?"

The guilt rises up in Mary's belly. The old guilt, the one that has yet to be broken into pieces, the one that sits like a glacier in her heart. She shakes her head again. No. She cannot say that this is unfair. It is a violation, it is a breach of trust, it is a flagrant abuse of an unspoken but clearly understood agreement. But it is not unjust. It is entirely, perfectly just.

She begins to cry as the object is pushed into her vagina.

It is certainly not how she had imagined her first time. For years, of course, she thought she would never have a first time; since she left the convent, she has begun to imagine the possibility. But this is not how she imagined it: bent over a desk, her clothes in disarray, her bare backside marked with vicious welts, weeping in pain and shame. It is entirely just. She lets the justice fill her, lets herself feel the enormity of her guilt, and the completely appropriate justice of what is happening to her. The object is hard and smooth, like plastic: it hurt when it first went in, but now it slides smoothly in and out, with no resistance.

"This is what happens to bad girls," Sister Catherine says through gritted teeth. "Bad girls have to let things be put inside them. Bad girls have to let themselves be touched in bad places, in ways they don't like.

Bad girls have to let their bodies be invaded and used by people who have power over them." Her voice has changed again. It is no longer solemn and punitive, nor is it gleefully sinister. It is a voice of quiet, carefully controlled rage. The object twists inside Mary at a savage angle. She flinches, and screams. She doesn't protest. She digs her fingers into the edge of the desk, and keeps as still as she can, and holds herself in place for her punishment.

"And bad girls," Sister Catherine says, "have to be made to feel things they don't want to feel." She slides the object out of Mary's vagina, and begins stroking her clitoris with it. Mary is aghast. She feels the way she did the time Sister Catherine made her drink the water and then beat her until she peed. She feels like she is going to burst, like she can't possibly allow herself do what she knows she will inevitably have to do. The object pushes back into her vagina, filling her anew with helplessness and humiliation; it then slides out and over her clitoris again, filling her with a different helplessness and humiliation, as she bucks her hips and rubs herself desperately against the object. The last strut on her self-control collapses, and the dam breaks. Her climax is forced into her body, and she receives it with shame and a desperate hope for forgiveness, as if her orgasm were the cane beating her backside, or the plastic object being pushed inside her.

Sister Catherine keeps swirling the object in slow circles on Mary's clitoris, until every last shudder has been forced out of Mary's body. She holds it in place for a minute longer, making Mary continue to feel it as she returns to reality. Then she sets it on the desk, and rests her hand on the small of Mary's back.

"I'm sorry I had to do that," she says. "But you had to learn." She always says this at the end of a punishment. She usually says it snarkily, the cruel voice pretending to be punitive. This time, she sounds like she means it.

"I know," Mary replies. "I am so sorry. You have no idea—I am so sorry. Please forgive me."

Catherine shakes her head. "It's not up to me to forgive. It's my job to make you feel repentance. Forgiveness is up to somebody else."

Mary nods, and wipes her eyes with the back of her hand. They stay in place for a long time, quietly. Finally Catherine pulls Mary's underwear back up, and pulls her skirt back down.

"So, I'll see you again next month? So we can continue your discipline?" Normally, Sister Catherine issues these words as a statement. A command, even. I'll see you again next month, so we can continue your discipline. This time, she asks, a bit tentatively.

Mary stays silent, praying for guidance. She is now more uncertain than ever about where this is going, or how it will end. This is taking a strange direction, a disturbing direction, leading to places she's frightened of, and to people she's not sure she wants to meet... or become.

But she knows she's not finished.

"Yes, Sister," she says, as she always does. "I'll be here when you say, to accept whatever discipline you consider necessary." She says the words "whatever discipline" with unusual emphasis.

"Good," Catherine says. She walks in front of Mary, still bent over the desk. She hands Mary a business card and puts her fingers over her lips.

"This is my home number," she murmurs under her breath. "Meet me there next week."

Mary nods, her face still wet. She fingers the card like a rosary. "Yes, Catherine. I'll go wherever you say."

Deprogramming

"How far do you want to go this time?"

"A little farther than last time."

"Last time we got almost to the belt. Are you sure you want to go farther? I don't think we can go farther without getting into the belt."

She nodded. "I know. It's okay. I don't want to, you know, go all the way with the belt. But I think I'd like to get started on it."

"You think." He took her hand. "You need to be more certain than that."

"Sorry." She took a deep breath. "Yes. I want to start on the belt today."

He let go of her hand and sat back, his arms folded across his belly like he was warding off a blow. "All right. So tell me that you want to do this."

"I.... Jesus, David, do I need to say this every time?"

"I need to hear it. Sarah... please. This is fucked up enough as it is. I can't do it if—"

She touched his knee. "Okay. It's okay." She folded her hands neatly in her lap, and spoke again..

"I want to do this. I am choosing to do this. And I know that I can stop it, any time I need to."

"And why do you want to do it?"

"I want to deal with what happened. I want to feel like I have some control over it. I want to move on." Her practiced voice began to wobble. "And... I want to get off. God help me, but this gets me off."

"Yeah, I know." He grinned weakly. "Me too. Fucked up, isn't it? Let's get started."

He stood up.

Eileen stood up. "Let's get started. Today's therapy group is now in session. Let the cleansing begin, in his holy name." She consulted a slip of paper. "Today we begin with the cleansing of Sarah. Sarah, please come to the center of the circle."

Sarah shivered. She'd known this was probably coming today. But knowing didn't help. Knowing didn't stop it from happening. She gritted her teeth, stood up from her metal folding chair, and walked to the center of the silent room, not knowing anything else she could do. She clenched her hands in front of her belly and waited.

"Sarah. You stand before the Tribe of the True Promise, your true family now and forever. And today you stand a failure. You have failed your father, Daddy John, and you have failed your family. You have spoken heresy, words against the teachings of Daddy John. You have mocked the teachings of Daddy John, in the hearing of your brothers and sisters. And you have pursued an unsanctioned erotic relationship, attempting to deceive Daddy John, without whom no true love is possible. Come forward for your punishment, and be cleansed of your shame."

The circle murmured. They're excited, Sarah thought bitterly. They can't wait. She felt a flash of anger, followed by an afterburn of shame. She'd been in the circle herself, twitching with anxious excitement as one of her brothers or sisters stepped forward to be punished. This whole thing is fucked up, she thought. Including me. Maybe I do deserve this.

She stepped forward to Eileen, who took her hands gently. "You have been shamed by Daddy John, and by me in his name," Eileen said. "Now you must shame yourself. Lower your trousers, and expose your body to your family, as Daddy John has exposed your sin."

"Pull down your pants," he said. "Your shame has been revealed. Now it's time to reveal your body,"

She unzipped her jeans and pulled them down with her panties, as quickly as she could, trying not to think about it. This was the worst part, she thought.

No, on second thought, it wasn't. But it was the hardest part. After this, it was out of her hands. Once she got past this, she didn't have to do anything, or decide anything—except whether to let it keep happening.

David sat down on the hard chair. "Now bend over my knee," he said. "You've acted like an irresponsible child, and you're going to be punished like a child." He paused. "You know I love you, right?"

She fumbled with the knot in her rough cotton drawstring pants, and let them fall to the floor, bowing her head. She wasn't wearing underwear. Daddy John said underwear was a sin. The murmuring of the circle grew louder: less anxious, more excited. She blushed and squeezed her eyes shut tight, feeling their eyes on her naked bottom. They're all going to watch, she thought, and none of them is going to stop it. They're all too relieved that it's not them this time. They're just going to watch the show.

Eileen sat down back on the hard chair. "Now bend over my knee," she said. "You've acted like an irresponsible child, and we have to punish you like a child. Daddy John loves you, and his punishment is a blessing. Now get over my knee."

The last sentence came out with a bite, a sharp detour from Eileen's usual soothing drone. Sarah had seen the results of that bite: the mass of bruises left on Jenny, and David, and little Shelley, Jesus, barely fifteen. She knew the gleeful cruelty behind that bite, slipping out through the cracks of the stern-but-loving mother routine. She was furious at the lie, and terrified at the truth behind it. She was powerless to do anything about either one.

She obeyed. There was nothing else she could do. She bent over Eileen's sturdy lap, praying to God, the one she no longer believed in, to let her leave her body and shut it all out.

"I know," Sarah said. "I love you too." She bent over his lap. His legs were thin and wiry, like a bird's. Breakable. She found it comforting.

Eileen rolled up her sleeves with a flourish. Someone in the circle whimpered, and immediately went silent. Eileen spoke. "My hand is the hand of Daddy John. You know Daddy's watching, don't you? He's always watching. Feel his hand on your body, and feel the pain of his disappointment."

It came down hard, sharp and hard like a sudden hailstorm. Sarah began screaming with the first blow, and kept screaming as the blows kept coming. She screamed with rage at Eileen and the lie of the loving mother; at Daddy John and the lie of the all-knowing father; at the trembling circle around her and the lie of the supportive family. She screamed at herself, for believing it for so long, for getting suckered into it in the first place. She screamed at her helplessness, her inability to make anything turn out different, ever. She screamed at her nonexistent God, for saying "No" to her prayers yet again, for making her stay in her body, making her feel the pain pounding down on her bare ass, and the malicious pleasure driving it, and the pathetic indignity it was forcing her to feel. The circle around her shifted in their seats, agitated and uncomfortable, as her screams rose in pitch from rage and protest to a panicked shriek.

And the blows kept coming, hard and fast and inescapable. She kept thinking it was going to stop, it had to stop, there was no way she could stand it if it kept coming, and it kept coming. It didn't matter if she could stand it or not.

"It's coming now," he said. "You're going to feel my hand, and my hand is going to punish you. It's going to hurt."

His first blow was light and gentle, almost a massage, she could barely feel it. She arched her back, welcoming it in: grateful for the gentleness now, grateful for the terrible pain she knew was coming, grateful for the sweet, gradual slide he was going to use to take her from here to there.

He began to turn up the heat, just a little, and she squirmed in anticipation. Her clit began to twitch, and she felt a familiar flutter of shame deep in her stomach. She got so excited when they did this. It was so fucked-up. She squirmed her hips harder, unnerved as always when the excitement began, trying to stave it off for just a moment more; but her squirming made her clit twitch harder, and she gave in with a gasp, and pushed her cunt hard against David's thigh, and let herself drop.

Her screams turned into sobs, weak and terrified. She squirmed hard, frantically trying to escape, to get just a little relief. She could hear the circle around her breathing harder; she knew she was giving them a show, screaming and crying and wiggling her bare backside like a whore. But she couldn't help it. She was helpless. She was without help.

It was getting harder now. And harder still. Harder than she really wanted; but of course, that was what she wanted. She wanted to feel helpless, to let herself go in the hands of someone she could trust.

She sank into the rhythm: fighting and giving in, fighting and giving in, surrendering to each new level of pain and surprising herself with how good it felt once she let it. Her clit was throbbing, demanding attention, and its hunger filled her consciousness.

But now it was really hard. Not just harder than she liked—harder than she could take. She tried, but she was only fighting now, just a struggle with no surrender. She pushed herself to take it for one last dreadful minute, and gave up at last. "Stop, David," she gasped. "It's too much. Please, God, fuck, stop it right now."

"I'm so sorry," she sobbed. "Please, stop. I'll never do it again, I swear. Just stop. I'm begging you."

The pain stopped at once. She let out a sigh of relief and shock at the unexpected mercy. But she heard Eileen's voice, cold and tight, and she began to sob again. She knew she hadn't stopped it. She had made it worse.

"You obviously don't understand," Eileen scolded. "You're obviously not sorry at all. If you were truly sorry, you wouldn't try to stop me. You'd understand that I need to punish you for as long as I see fit. You'd understand that a disobedient child can't decide for herself how much she should be

punished. You'd be ashamed of yourself, and you'd welcome this punishment as a chance to cleanse your shame."

Eileen shook her head sadly. "We obviously need to take this further. Stand up, and take off my belt."

He stopped immediately. He rested his hand on her warm bottom for a long time. He watched her back until it relaxed, listened to her breath until it quieted. Then he spoke, his voice serious and full of sorrow.

"I have to take my belt off now, Sarah. I'm sorry. But it's time. I have to do this."

Sarah froze.

Fuck, no, she thought. Please, God. Not the belt.

Eileen cleared her throat. "You disappoint me, Sarah. You've never had to be cleansed before. I'd hoped you'd take it better than this. But you obviously have plenty of willfulness left in you. Selfish, childish willfulness. You think you can defy me? You think you know better than me what's right for you?" Her voice was cracking again. "Think again, Sarah. David, come over here and take off my belt." She smirked. "You've done it often enough, David, you should be good at it by now."

She held herself perfectly still, terrified, trying to disappear. She heard someone, David she assumed, stand up and move toward her from out of the circle. She felt him fiddle quickly with Eileen's belt buckle, pull the belt out of her belt loops, fold it up and hand it to her. She heard him move back to his place in the circle without a word. She felt pity for him. She suddenly understood what people meant when they said, "This is going to hurt me more than it hurts you."

She heard Eileen smack the belt into her open hand, and the sound drove David out of her mind, and drove the fear and paralysis back in.

"Now stand up," Eileen instructed. "I'm going to stand up as well. When I do, put your hands on the seat of the chair. And then wait. When it begins, you may make as much noise as you like, and you may move your body as much as you like..." "—Eileen paused here, and shivered at her own

words—*"but you may not move your hands from the chair, or your feet from the ground, until I say we're done."*

She nodded. "I know. It's okay. I'm ready."

"All right then. Stand up. Put your hands on the chair. I'm going to stand behind you, and I'm going to beat you with the belt until I'm done."

She complied.

She was shaking with pain, and with fear. She was weak with shame at the staring eyes upon her, and with anger at the faces behind the eyes. She could barely stand up. But she complied.

She knew there was nothing she could do. Anything she did to try to stop it would just make it worse: would bring on the switch, or the wooden paddle, or the belt until she bled and passed out. The only thing that would stop it was to let it happen.

So she let it happen. She stood up, and bent over, her hands on the chair, her bare, trembling bottom in the air, her cotton drawstring pants crumpled around her ankles, the Tribe of the True Promise sitting in a circle around her, gaping like zombies.

And she let it happen. She glued her hands to the chair and her feet to the floor, letting herself obey the woman who was breathing hard and smacking the belt into her hand to build the suspense. She arched her back to give a prettier target, and waited patiently, passively, for the first blow to land.

And she let herself be beaten with the belt.

She screamed obediently when it landed. And as the blows kept landing, she kept screaming, a gift for the woman who panted behind her like a dog as she gleefully whipped her raw. She screamed and wept, and she wiggled her bottom and jiggled her dangling tits, shaking her flesh like a stripper, letting herself obey the unspoken orders as well as the spoken ones.

And she let herself feel ashamed. She knew that was what Eileen wanted most of all, that Eileen wouldn't stop until she got it. So she gave it to her.

It wasn't the right shame, though. Not the shame Eileen was looking for. It wasn't shame at her blasphemy or disobedience; it wasn't even shame at being stripped and humiliated and punished on her bare bottom in front of her whole family.

Her shame was that she had let this happen. Her shame was that she was weak and stupid: too stupid to see how bad things were until they had gotten too bad to leave, too weak to pull it together and leave when they did get really bad. Her shame was that she had no power, that she'd given away what little she had, if she'd ever had any at all. Her shame was that she was here—screaming, squirming, wiggling her bare ass like a bitch in heat for the woman who was beating it raw—because she had put herself here.

And her shame was that she had let this happen to her brothers and sisters. She had sat in the circle like they were sitting now, half-petrified, half-leering. She had stared with fear and relief and fascination, as David or Shelley or some other Godforsaken soul pulled down their pants and put their exposed bodies under Eileen's hands.

She deserved this punishment. She deserved this shame. She sank into it, and let it seep into her muscles and bones, and pulled it up by handfuls to give to Eileen.

It was the wrong shame. But she knew Eileen would never know the difference. Shame was shame to Eileen: the woman was actually moaning now, supposedly with the effort of beating Sarah's ass at full speed and full strength.

Sarah sank deeper into the pain and the shame, and whimpered louder, and jiggled her tits and ass harder. She splayed open her bent knees to give a glimpse in between them... and Eileen grunted at last, a long series of animal grunts like a pig rooting in a trough, and collapsed to the floor, dropping the belt.

"Praise be to Daddy John," she cried. "I feel his forgiveness. Do you feel it too, child? Do you know he's watching? Do you know how happy he is right now? Feel the shame lifted out of your heart. You're free now."

She obeyed.

She felt it now: the helplessness she'd been waiting for. She moved like she was in a trance: standing up, waiting for David to move into place behind her, placing her hands on the chair and shifting her feet into position. She waited, patient and afraid, her bare bottom tingling in memory and anticipation.

He struck, and she gasped in shock. Oh, fuck. She'd forgotten how much the belt hurt. So much harder than the hand, and more cold. So much not about human contact; so purely about the cruelty, and the pain.

But she knew she'd asked for this. Literally. Just a few minutes ago. And she knew she needed it. She just couldn't remember why right now. It hurt too much. The belt cut into her ass, the pain exploding onto her skin like a bomb and then radiating through her flesh into her clit and her cunt. He was hitting her slowly, and hard, letting her feel each blow, giving it time to blossom and fade, giving her time to recover. And time to feel the next one.

She began to cry. Not a yelping cry of protest, but a soft weeping rain of despair, and of giving in.

He kept beating her; close together now, hard and heartless, his teeth gritted with the struggle to finish. Then he dropped the belt to the floor with a clatter, and grabbed her around her waist.

"I said you're free now." The woman was smirking condescendingly. "That means you can move again. And you can cover yourself." Her smirk widened into a sneer. "Unless you'd rather stay like that, of course."

Sarah stood up. She swayed for a moment, from the rush of the blood back to her head, and the flood of relief that she wasn't willing to trust. She pulled up her pants and fiddled with the strings, finally managing to tie them again. She wobbled back to her place in the circle and sat down, dropping her eyes, avoiding the stares of the circle around her, cringing at the touch of the metal folding chair. Eileen turned away from her. She had already moved on.

"All right," she said cheerily. "I think we have time for one more cleansing. Let's look at Daddy's list…" She peered at the slip of paper. "Ah. David again, I see." She clucked her tongue. "Such a disappointment. So many times. David, will you ever be truly clean of your shame?"

David stood up casually. "Okay. Sure. Whatever." Sarah listened for defiance in his voice, but heard only defeat.

She caught his eye. She had to give him something, something to hang on to. And now she knew what. She caught his eye, and nodded her head, just a flicker, barely perceptible even to him.

Yes, she said. Tonight. She'd said No before. She was weak, and frightened. But now she knew. Now she was free. Now she was ready to leave.

"It's over," he said. "It's all over."

She crumpled to the floor, and he crumpled with her, holding her around the shoulders as tightly as he could. She leaned into his thin chest, cried like the newly widowed, and pushed her hand between her legs. He held her as she made herself come. She came fast and hard, frantically flicking her clit with her finger, clenching his hand with her other fist, still weeping onto his shoulder.

Her tears dissipated with her shudders, and she relaxed at last, curling up on the floor with her head in his lap. He stroked her hair, watched her back until it relaxed, listened to her breath until it quieted. She spoke at last. "Okay," she said. "Thank you."

"That was okay?"

"Yeah."

"I didn't push it too far?"

"No. It was perfect. You pushed it just far enough."

"And you're okay now."

She patted his hand. "Yeah. I'm back. Thanks."

He squeezed her hand, and kissed it. Then he reached back to pick up the belt, and handed the belt to her.

She nodded. "Right. How far do you want to go this time?"

The Rest Stop

He pulls his pickup truck into the rest stop. It's one in the morning on a weeknight. The rest stop isn't a happenstance place where he stopped to catch some sleep before moving on. It's his destination.

Nobody else is there yet. But another truck that had been behind him on the highway pulls in after him. He ducks his head, prays to God for forgiveness, then flashes his lights. A specific sequence of shorts and longs, signaling what he's here for: signaling generally, and then more particularly, what he's here for. A sequence he now knows intimately. A sequence he sometimes has nightmares about.

The truck behind him flashes back.

He gets out of his truck, goes into the men's room, walks over to the metal sink. He bends over it, braces himself with his hands. He waits. He tries to pretend that he isn't here for what he's here for; that he's just pulling over at a rest stop to wash his face, and that what's about to happen will be a shock, nothing he planned for, against his will. The fact that he has inserted lube into his asshole with a syringe makes this pretense impossible. He waits.

The man walks in behind him.

He shudders, more in fear than anticipation. He knows that the man could be dangerous. Bad things—worse than what he's already doing—could happen. Bad things have already happened. He's been hurt: some of these men are rough, rougher than he likes. He's been torn, before he learned about the lube. He's had his wallet stolen. One guy took off his belt and beat his ass with it before he fucked him. The guy must have gotten his signals wrong; or maybe he just didn't care, maybe the guy was a genuine psycho. He stood there, bent over at the sink, and took it. He hadn't been belted since he was a kid, it hurt like the fires of Judgment, tears poured down his face as the belt landed on his ass again and again, and he gripped the sink tighter and gritted his teeth and let it happen. The man finally pushed his cock into him, and the burning pain on the skin of his ass felt clean, like it balanced out the sinful shame of the hard cock he'd invited inside. He felt like he deserved it. He felt like maybe God would have mercy on him on Judgment Day, if He remembered the welts that were on his ass when this man's cock was pushing inside it.

He never used to get off on pain and shame. As sick as he was, as sick as he knows this thing is, that was never his sickness. But now, after years of getting fucked too hard in rest stop bathrooms, his body has been trained. The shame he feels about his lusts, and the repulsive places he goes to fulfill them, and the disgraceful, sometimes painful things he lets happen to him, are now hopelessly tangled up with the lust itself. The night that he got beaten with the belt, he went on the Internet afterward, and looked up the headlight code for "beat me first." He hasn't used it yet, but he always thinks about it.

This man, tonight, now comes up behind him. The man sets a hand on his shoulder—warm, weirdly reassuring. Then the hands come around his waist, and undo his belt, and pull down his trousers and his shorts. He feels the familiar throb in his cock, and the familiar shame, as his ass and his cock are exposed, and this thing he's doing becomes unmistakably what it is. He spread his legs and waits. The man clears his throat.

Oh, Jesus have pity, no. A talker. Usually all this takes place in total silence. But some of them like to talk. They tell him what a slut he is; they ask him how he likes their big cocks in his pussyhole; they tell him fantasies about the disgusting perverted things they want to do to him. He desperately wishes they wouldn't. He feels like he has no defense against their words: his armor is down, he is bent over a men's room sink in a filthy rest stop with his pants pulled down, getting fucked in the ass or about to get fucked, and whatever they say goes right into the core of his soul.

The man speaks.

"God, I want you.

"You are so fucking hot, do you know that? Such a tight little ass, and such tight wiry legs, and those gorgeous hands. You are amazing. I want you so much. I can't wait to fuck you."

The words are painful. The man's admiration makes him flinch, more than any filthy fantasies he's had to listen to. The words make him feel like... he doesn't want to think about what they make him feel like. The voice is faintly familiar. Someone from local TV or radio, maybe. It wouldn't be the first time. The voice goes on.

"I love how dirty this is, don't you? I love that all over the world, men are having dirty fantasies about this, and here we are actually doing it. It's so fucking hot."

He feels the hands on him again. On his bare ass, squeezing and fondling; he braces himself and spreads his legs wider. But then the hands wander: down to caress his thighs, up and over to rub his shoulders, pulling his shirt up to play with his nipples and fondle his chest.

He hates it when they do this. It makes him feel... he doesn't want to think about it. Like a faggot. The word jumps into his mind, and won't be pushed back. He despises it, he struggles against it. But this man's hands are hard to resist: strong, calloused, and at the same time intelligent and curious: exploring his body, seeking out his hot spots, lingering when they find a good one and then teasing away to search for another. He shudders. He normally just stands still and silent and lets himself get fucked; but he can't help it, he begins to moan, and to squirm. God help him, he wants this so much.

"God, I want you," the man says. "Say it."

He shakes his head. He can't. He'll come here, he'll flash the lights, he'll bend over the sink and offer his ass to be fucked. But he can't say out loud that he wants it. If he does, he'll be lost.

The man's fingers toy at the opening of his asshole: teasing, lingering, making him squirm and buck. "Come on. Say it."

He feels like he's drowning. He clutches on to the last shreds of his soul, keeping him afloat. The man's fingers are circling his asshole, widening the rip in his life raft, pulling him down. He struggles, and sinks.

"Please," he says. "Yes. I want you."

A finger goes in, not even an inch, then pulls out again. "You want me to what. Say it. Tell me what you want me to do."

His mouth is dry. "I want you to fuck me."

The finger goes in deeper. A second one joins it. "Say it again. Keep talking. Tell me that you want me. Tell me what you want me to do."

He's falling now, and the momentum of his fall makes every word come easier. "Please," he says. "Please keep fingering me. And then... fuck me in the ass. Please slide your hard cock into my asshole. God, I want your cock in me so much. Please fuck me, make me come with your cock deep inside me." All the words he could never say out loud, all the words he could barely stand to think, he says now to this man. He knows the words are dirty, but they pour out of him like a firehose of clean water clearing out a sewer pipe. The man fingers him, and then slides his cock in: gentle, and nasty. The words gushing out of him begin to mix with moans, and gibberish.

He reaches down as he babbles, and grips his cock. He never does this. He always waits for the other guy to jerk him off; or he waits for the guy to leave, and jerks himself off in the toilet, alone. But now he licks his hand and strokes his cock, still begging out loud for the fucking that he's getting, matching his rhythm to the cock stroking inside him. The guy starts to talk again. "Yeah, that's right. Jerk yourself off while I fuck you. That's good. That is so right. God, I can feel you squeezing around me. God, that's..." They are both gibbering now, talking over each other, their words and grunts overlapping, intertwining. He feels the man straining, and then coming, the careful seductive rhythm switching to a hard frenzy deep inside him. It triggers a blown fuse in his brain. His moans rise in pitch to a wail of despair, and he comes into his hand, the man's cock still inside his ass.

His cum drips off his hand onto the foul rest stop floor. The man takes his hand and squeezes, smearing the cum onto both their fingers. The man pulls out of his ass, tugs on his hand, turns him around to face him.

He's never looked any of these men in the face. He looks at this one now.

Fuck.

He knows him. Paul. From his parish. Paul, who he sees at church every Sunday. Paul, whose mother is on the church building committee with his wife Adele. A few years younger than him, solid guy, good looking, everyone always wondered why he didn't marry. Christ. That's why his voice sounded familiar. Merciful God, he thinks, please forgive me. Paul seems oblivious to his horror. Paul gives him a wide grin: happy, and unsurprised.

"I saw your truck pull in," Paul says. "I recognized it, but I couldn't believe it was you. I've been looking at you for you so long, I never thought—my God. I so need to see you again. Not here. When can we meet? There's a motel down near the city. A place I know about. They won't care."

He shakes his head. This was bad enough already. He can't go any further. He can't go there, to that motel, with this man that he likes, with this man whose name he knows. He can't be what this man wants him to be. "I'm sorry, Paul. No. I don't—I'm not a faggot."

Every man who has ever fucked him here, who has said anything about it at all, has said that they're not a faggot. The man who beat his ass with a belt before he fucked him said afterwards that he wasn't a faggot. Paul strokes his cheek, looks at him with pity and compassion.

"Yes. You are. You're a faggot.

"You are a faggot, Albert. I am a faggot. And I want to see you again. I am a faggot, I am a gay man, and I want to suck your cock, and play with your nipples, and massage your ass until you beg me to fuck you. I want you to tell me every sexy thing you've ever thought about, and I want to do it with you. Don't—Albert, you come here. You must have been coming here for I don't know how long. You're a faggot. I'm a faggot. Who cares. When can I see you again?"

He'd been right.

This man was dangerous.

He has just been fucked in the ass, and his pants are still down, and he has no defense against Paul's words. His armor is gone. The words that Paul is saying go right into the core of his soul.

He is a faggot.

He reaches out to grip Paul's hair by the back of the head. He leans in and kisses him, soft, and deep. He can feel Paul's surprise, and joy, spring up in the man's body like a sapling. He clutches Paul close, and presses against him, and their softening cocks rub together along with their tongues. He has been coming to this place, and to places like it, for thirteen years. He has never kissed another man before today.

He finally breaks away. "Wednesdays," he says. "I usually come here on Wednesdays. Tell me the name of the motel."

SWEET STUFF

Dear Marla

To: Marla (marlabird@thistlebooks.com)
From: Chris (clv@compufix.com)
Subject: I miss you

Dear Marla,

I miss you. The flight went smoothly and my family is relatively sane, except Fran who's having fits about Mom's birthday being perfect. I guess I didn't help matters by calling her Franny-Fat-Fanny, which after thirty-odd years still makes her yell at me. I'm sorry you couldn't be here to see it.

This is what I'm thinking about you today. I'm remembering something I read once, about how 95% of sex scenes in movies show the couple having sex for the first time. I don't know if they meant that number literally or were making it up to make a point. But I realized that I don't get that. I know all these guys (women too, probably) who get bored doing it with the same person, who need a fresh body every few months or years to keep their attention. But I don't get it. I've never gotten it. It seems so ridiculously obvious to me that sex gets better with time, not worse. It's like playing the piano. You need to practice, for years. You can't play the piano for a few months and then quit and switch to the tuba, and then quit that and play the saxophone for a while. Not if you're going to be really good at it.

When I'm going down on you, for example. (What a nice example.) There's a spot, I don't know how to describe where it is, it's on the right side of your nub, kind of high up at the top. When I'm licking you, if you're tensing up and I can tell you're ready to come but don't want to yet, if I lick that spot you kind of relax. and go to this other place, this place that's blissful and peaceful and sort of like an orgasm but not one. All that shark-like forward motion stops, for both of us, and it's like sitting still for a moment in the woods. Until I move, over to one of your serious hot spots, just a millimeter down is all it takes, and you start squirming again.

And those hot spots, for another example. When we were first going out, I'd stumble on one and you'd jump out of your skin, and I'd think, Aha! Money in the bank. And I'd zero in on it and make you crazy for about ten seconds, and then a second later you'd get kind of numb and irritable, and we'd be back to square one. Now I know. It is like money in the bank, but I can't spend it all right away or it'll be gone. I know I need to tease it, court it, circle around it, pass my tongue over it for just a quarter of a second and then move away. I know I need to get you worked up, missing it, wanting it, before I come back to it again, for half a second this time, just a couple of hard flicks with the tip of my tongue before I slip off again. I know I can't zero in on it until you're making your final run. And I know that once I do start zeroing in, once you've got your momentum going, I absolutely can't stop.

I didn't know any of this seven years ago. I didn't know a lot of it four years ago. And if I'd dropped you after six months for someone with different colored hair or a different bra size, I'd never have found out. It's an awful thought. I can't stand thinking about it.

It's not like I know things, so now I can go down on you the right way, the same way, every time. It's like, I know things, so I can mix them up, play with them, shuffle the deck in a different way. I can creep up on a hot spot slow and steady like a glacier, or I can flick at it and flick away and then flick back again, or I can dance around it all night and drive you crazy, make you wonder if I'm ever going to get there. I can run my fingers up and down your lips, or use my fingers to spread you apart and open you up so your clit can't get away, or put one inside you for that sensory overload thing that makes you so twitchy. I can press your thighs apart and hold them there, firmly and just a little roughly, like a manly-but-sensitive hero in a romance novel; or I can stroke them on the inside with the tips of my fingers, a light brushing, almost subliminal, adding a bit of background and complexity to the picture I'm drawing on your pussy with my tongue.

It's always new. Always a different mix. The time we did it at Dinosaur National Park, giggling and trying to stay quiet and bumping into the tent poles. That time we called in sick and spent the day in bed together, ordering take-out and watching videos and having sex all day. The night before my father's funeral. Last night before you drove me to the airport. Every time is different.

And that's just going down on you.

Anyway, it's a moving target. You change, I change. Our bodies, our thoughts, our desires. The minute I think I know you, you come up with some dirty new idea, or remember some dirty old idea that's been in the back of your mind for years and now can't wait another second. And I'm dying of curiosity. I can't wait to find out whatever new thing it is I'm going to learn seven years from now, or three months from now, or a week from now when I get home.

All of which is a long-winded way to say that I love you, and I miss you, and I wish you were here to try all this long-winded theory with in person. I'll write again in a day or two. I'll see you in a week. Keep the hot spots burning.

Love,
Chris

Doing It Over

I was seventeen years old the first time that a lover hit me on the ass and asked me if I liked it.

Well, okay, he wasn't a lover. He was really just some guy I'd picked up on the street; just some guy I'd smiled at, who smiled back and bought me ice cream and took me home. Just some guy I'd fucked and fucked and fucked, for hours and hours, in every position we could think of, until the skin of his dick was rubbed raw and I could barely walk. It doesn't matter who he was. What matters is what I said when he hit me on the ass and asked me if I liked it.

What I said was No.

No, I don't want to do that, I lied. I'm not into that.

He backed off immediately. I'm not into that stuff either, he lied.

And I spent the rest of that night, and all the rest of the nights we spent together, thinking to myself: Tell him you changed your mind. Tell him you want to try it. You know he really wants to; you know he'll do it if you ask him. Go ahead. Ask him. I spent the rest of that night, and all the rest of the nights we spent together, trying to find the courage to change my mind...and failing.

So now I want a second chance. I want to tell the story the way I wish it had come out. I want to do it over again.

* * *

He smacks me on the ass. Quite lightly, really. "Do you like that?" he asks.

130

I stiffen. The temperature in my stomach drops about fifteen degrees. I don't even think about my answer; it comes out like a reflex, like kicking when the doctor hits your knee in just the right spot.

"No," I answer coldly. "I'm not into that."

He backs off immediately. "I'm not into that stuff either," he says.

I know he's lying. I know he's just trying to save face. He doesn't want me to think he's a pervert who's into weird shit like that. He doesn't want me not to like him; he doesn't want me to stop fucking him. But I know he wants to do it. This is my chance. After all these years, after all those hours I spent thinking and thinking and thinking about it, this is my chance to actually try it. And I just blew it.

He rubs my lower back for a moment, easing some of the tension out of me and some of the trust back in, then runs his hands down the backs of my thighs and opens my legs. He wets his fingers with his mouth and slides them over my clit and into my cunt, over my clit and into my cunt. It feels really good; I arch my back and move my hips in circles and make little groaning noises. But I'm not really thinking about his fingers between my legs. I'm thinking about his hand on my ass. And I'm so scared I can't speak.

* * *

Wait a minute. Do I want this to be about fear? That's what it was about the first time. If I'm going to re-tell this, maybe I should do it without the fear.

* * *

He smacks me on the ass. Quite lightly, really. It startles me; it tingles, wakes me up. My entire attention is focused on the imprint of his hand on my skin.

"Do you like that?" he asks.

"Mmmmm," I say. "I think so. Why don't you do it again?"

* * *

No. That doesn't work at all. It's false, unnatural. It doesn't make sense for me not to be afraid. Let me try again.

* * *

He smacks me on the ass. Quite lightly, really. "Do you like that?" he asks.

I stiffen, and don't even think about my answer. "No," I answer coldly. "I'm not into that."

He backs off immediately. "I'm not into that stuff either," he says hastily.

He rubs my back for a moment, easing some of the tension out of me and some of the trust back in, then runs his hands down my thighs and opens my legs. He wets his fingers with his mouth and slides them over my clit and into my cunt. But I'm not really thinking about his fingers between my legs. I'm not even paying attention. All I'm thinking about is his hand on my ass. All my attention, all my sensation, is focused on the imprint of his hand on my skin. And I'm so scared I can't speak.

What is it I'm afraid of? It isn't him; we've been fucking for hours, and he hasn't done one thing that I didn't want him to do, and he's stopped on a dime every time I've said No.

"Wait a minute," I say. "I think..." I shut my lips tight over my teeth.

* * *

Jesus. This is harder than I thought. I'm finding it almost impossible to imagine it. Having the courage to try this at seventeen? I'd have had to have been a completely different person.

But that's why I find this so compelling. It's why I can't forget this story, why I want so badly to tell it over and have it come out right. It isn't just a missed opportunity for a spanking; God knows I've had enough of those in my lifetime. It isn't that one spanking that I want. It's all the others that could have come after it. It's the missed years, the years I spent from seventeen to twenty-five wondering and wishing and trying to get up the nerve to ask someone else. It's being the person I'd be now if I'd spent those years knowing I was a pervert instead of being scared to death that I might be; being the person I'd be now if I hadn't spent eight years hoping that someone else would hit me while they fucked me, and trying to screw up the courage to say so.

* * *

I'm not really thinking about his fingers between my legs. I can't even pay attention to that. All I'm thinking about is his hand on my ass. All my attention, all my sensation, is focused on the imprint of his hand on my skin. All I can think about is the leftover tingling on that one spot, the sharp feeling that's fading out of my body even as it's expanding inside my head. And I'm so scared I can't even speak.

So what is it I'm so afraid of? It isn't him; he hasn't done one thing I didn't want him to do, and he's stopped on a dime every time I've said No.

So I guess what I'm afraid of is...well, what if I like it? What if I like it a lot? What if I like it even better than I like fucking? What sort of person does that make me, anyway? What if I'm the sort of person who thinks about getting hurt every time she plays with herself, who thinks about getting her face slapped and her arms pinned to the bed every time she gets fucked? What if I'm the sort of person who actually *likes* feeling sore and raw and barely able to walk after she's been fucking all night? What if I'm the sort of person who gets slapped on the ass when she's fucking and can't think about anything else?

But I already know that. It's too late now. I am that sort of person. So...

"Wait a minute," I say.

He slides his fingers out of my cunt at once. "What is it, baby?" he asks, his voice smooth and sweet like custard. "Are you too sore? Do you want me to do something else?"

I shake my head. "It isn't that."

He strokes the insides of my thighs, gently, patiently, seductively. "Mmm hmmm?" he prompts.

Just say it, I think. All you have to do is say it.

"When you—you know, hit me on my ass, a minute ago?"

He draws a sharp breath, wary, tense, hopeful. "Yeah?"

I close my eyes, breathe in, and open them again. "I think..." I shut my lips tight over my teeth.

"Yeah?"

I shudder, and breathe again. "I think... I think I wanna try that."

* * *

Okay. There we go. Much better.

* * *

I shudder, and breathe again. "I think... I think I wanna try that."

He sucks in his breath, an inward hiss, almost a gasp. "I thought you said you weren't into that."

Defensive and uncomfortable, tense and embarrassed, I snap my legs together. "I know what I said," I answer. "I just... I dunno. Forget it. Forget I said anything."

He strokes my butt and the backs of my thighs. "Hey, it's okay," he says smoothly. "Yeah, sure. I'm into it. I mean... I could be into it. Sure. Let's do it."

I look at him over my shoulder and narrow my eyes. "I thought you said you weren't into that stuff."

"Well, so did you, baby," he retorts, the pitch of his voice rising like a penny whistle. "You said you didn't want to do it. I don't get you. What do you want, anyway?"

"I know what I said," I snap...

* * *

Ah, shit. This is going nowhere. We could spend all night doing this.

* * *

I shudder, and breathe again. "I think... I think I wanna try that."

He sucks in his breath sharply. "I thought you said you weren't into that."

Defensive and uncomfortable, tense and embarrassed, I wrap my arms around my chest and start stroking my shoulders. "I know what I said," I answer. "I just... I dunno. I was spooked. I don't know what I want."

He strokes my butt and the backs of my thighs. "Hey, it's okay," he says. "Yeah, sure. I'm into it. I mean... I might be into it. You wanna do it, you don't wanna do it? Whatever. Just tell me. If you wanna do it... you know, I could do it. If you want to."

"Well," I gulp, "I think... yeah. Sure. Let's try it."

He slaps me on the ass again. Same spot. Just a wee bit harder this time. "How's that?"

I draw a deep, shuddering breath, and relax. My legs fall open an inch wider. A drop of come—mine or his, I'm not sure—leaks out of my sore, swollen cunthole and trickles down slowly over my clit.

"That's good," I say. "Yeah. I think I like that." I let out a deep sigh, and stretch out my arms above my head, and arch my back for the next blow.

Open

When it started, it seemed pretty reasonable. Manageable.

It's still manageable. Just in a different way now.

It started as something she liked to do in bed, with her lovers. A simple request: "Spread me open."

She wanted her pussy lips spread wide apart. As wide as they could go. Or she wanted to be asked—or be told—to spread her lips apart herself. She wanted to open herself, or be opened... and she wanted to be looked at. To be seen.

It moved on. She started asking her lovers to take pictures of her, showing her pussy, spreading herself open. Then she started taking pictures of herself. Then she started putting the pictures on the Internet.

And then she got the Webcam.

At first, she was doing it for free. She got a cheapo website. She'd put up a notice when she felt like going on, to give her audience a heads-up. She'd turn the camera on.

And she'd climb onto the table.

She would already be naked. This wasn't about a tease. Her audience didn't want a tease. They wanted to see her cunt, wide open and ready right now. And she wanted her cunt to be seen, right now. So she would climb onto the table. She would lie on her back and spread her legs. And she would show her pussy.

In every way she could think of.

She knew how to give a show. She didn't just lie back and open her legs. She had a hundred different ways to spread her legs wide and show her pussy. It was all she thought about when she jerked off. And the fact that she now had an audience fired her imagination even more.

She spread her pussy with her fingers. She spread her pussy with clips, little ones attached to thin chains: she would clip them onto her outer lips, and pull the chains apart, and tug her lips apart to open up her hole. She got a series of dildos—clear ones, glass and acrylic, so she could fuck herself and still give an unobstructed view between her legs. She got a sort of sling, a contraption that bound her ankles and anchored behind her neck, and that pulled her feet high and wide in the air. She got on all fours, and raised her ass in the air like a dog in heat, and showed off her pussy from behind.

She would never just lie there. She would wriggle and moan, play with her tits, put things into her mouth. She would play with her clit until she screamed and came... always careful to keep her fingers high and out of the way, covering up as little as possible, always keeping her hole carefully on display. She would squirm her hips from side to side, or pump her pussy into the air like it was getting fucked by the Holy Spirit.

And she would talk. She would tell her audience what a dirty girl she was. She would tell them how horny she was, how excited it made her when they looked at her pussy. She would tell them how wet she was, and then put her finger in her pussy to show them. She would beg to be fucked, to be punished, to be spread open even wider.

She meant every word.

She got an audience. A big one. Word of Web spread: hundreds, then thousands.

And she decided: What the hell. She didn't go to business school for nothing.

She put out a call for models. She'd need a lot of them to keep the site going 24/7; but she didn't have to pay that much. The economy sucked, and it was easy work, easier than standard porn. The girls didn't need to fuck anybody, or memorize lines, or anything like that. All they needed to do was be naked, with their legs spread, live on camera.

Of course, the more they did, the better. She paid bonuses for girls who drew a big audience, girls with fans and regular viewers. That's how she kept things interesting, kept the girls from just getting on their backs and flopping their legs open for an hour. She wasn't just concerned about her business, either. She was concerned about her reputation. She was concerned about keeping her audience. And she liked to watch the show, too. She wanted the show to be hot for her own sake. She was her own best customer.

So she'd let go of the girls who didn't do that much... and she'd give bonuses to the ones who did. The girls who spread their legs and told dirty stories. The girls who spread their legs and gave deep- throat blowjobs to dildos. The girls who took requests: who spread their legs, and then did the things their fans had asked them to do in email. The girls who spread their legs and talked about how helpless they were, how anyone who walked in could just take advantage of them. The girls who spread their legs and talked about what sluts they were, how anyone who walked in could count on getting fucked within an inch of their life. The girls who spread their legs and begged to be taken and used. The girls who spread their legs and spanked themselves, on their thighs and on their pussies. She got some of her best show ideas from her girls.

She lost some viewers when she started to charge money. But most of them loved it. They loved her. They loved what she was doing... and now they didn't have to wait for her unpredictable appearances. Her rates were reasonable... and now, any time of the day, any day of the week, they could see a girl, live, with her legs spread wide and every centimeter of her pussy easily on view.

And pretty often, that girl was her.

Now that she didn't have a day job, she could do this whenever she wanted. And she wanted to a lot. Her girls mostly liked the work, but they did gripe that the boss lady always took the primo time slots. She'd even bump them from the schedule when she got the itch: pay them off, tell them, "Thanks, you can go home, I got this one. " And she would strip down, then and there, and climb up onto her table. She never bothered with costumes: she liked the girls who did, as long as they didn't cover up anything important. But she never did herself. She only ever wanted to be naked.

She's thought about expanding her show a little, branching out into some new areas. She's thought about playing out some scenarios: doctor's exams, alien probes, that sort of thing. She's thought about getting an actual cameraman: someone who could move around, do closeups, zoom in between her legs at crucial moments. She's thought about getting some of her girls to hold her down and spread her open: pin her hands and shoulders to the table, push her thighs apart, get their fingers in there and force her pussy into the open. She likes that idea: having hands all over her body, all there to pin her like a butterfly in a case and put her hole on display like a flower. A dozen or more hands obsessively devoted to her exposure.

But she's not sure. All that could turn this into just another porno site. Plus all that would call for acting... and she hates the bad acting in porno videos. She wants to keep this special. And she wants to keep it real.

Besides, she wants to keep a few things on reserve. She's already taken this pretty far, almost as far as she can. She wants a little something left, something she's still covered up. She doesn't want to open all her presents at once. She wants to keep a few wrapped up, so she can open them later.

So right now, she's not going to do that. Right now, she's just going to climb up onto her table. It's Saturday night, her biggest night, and she has a big show planned: two full hours, with toys, and yoga poses, and special requests, and a dirty story to tell that she's been jerking off to all week. She lies back, and spreads her legs, and starts the show.

A Live One

What an asshole, Sheila thinks as she plays with her pussy. He's been popping quarters into the booth like they were rock candy. A smile wouldn't cost anything extra.

She smiles down at the customer through the glass, a sugary, seductive smile full of bubble and promise. He responds with the same blank stare he's been giving her for the last five minutes. His face is flat and listless, a cheap cement statue of a gloomy frog, with a faint trickle of hostility leaking through the stone set of his mouth.

She sighs and spins around, giving up, turning her face away. She sticks her butt in the window and runs her hand slowly over her ass. The fucking brick-wall men, she thinks. I've never understood why they come here. I mean, I can give them the sight of a dancing naked woman, but I can't give them the joy of watching a naked woman dance. Don't they get that they have to bring that themselves?

She licks her forefinger and runs it up and down her pussy as she gyrates her hips to the thumping music. She catches Tanisha's eye and gives her the contemptuous look she can't give the customer. Tanisha gives a quick nod of sympathy and turns back to Danielle. The younger girl is sprawled over Tanisha's lap; she squirms and rolls her hips dramatically, putting on an extravagant show for the two drunken sailors in the corner booth. Tanisha scowls ferociously and slaps Danielle's tight, round rump; Danielle gives a theatrical squeal and wriggles in delight.

I like a girl who enjoys her work, Sheila smiles to herself. She knows these two; they'll be doing the real thing later on. They love faking the guys out, but they never do it for real for money.

She hears the panel slide down behind her, and glances over her shoulder. Yup, he's gone. What a tragic loss to the human race. She arches her back, sore from bending over, and looks around dutifully for a new customer.

Sure enough, just as she finishes stretching, the panel in the other corner booth slides up. She glances at Lorelei, who's busily spreading her pussy for a middle-aged man with a briefcase in one hand and his dick in the other. Guess the new one's mine, Sheila concludes. Conscientious as always, she shimmies over, squats in front of the guy, and smiles. "Hi," she hollers over the deafening synth-pop din. "I'm Chloe."

In response, he pulls a pad and pen out of his pocket and begins scribbling. He holds it up to the window and smiles back. *Hi Chloe,* it reads. *I'm Henry.*

Her eyebrows shoot up, surprised and impressed. Smart guy, she thinks. Inventive. And he actually wants to talk to me. Maybe this will be a live one.

She tucks her legs under her like a cheesecake model and runs her hand over her torso. "So, Henry; you come here often?"

He writes furiously and holds the pad up again. *Yes,* it says. *That's why I brought this. I know it's too loud in there for you to hear me...*

He flips to another page and scribbles some more. *But I want to be able to talk. This is the best I could come up with.*

He reaches into his pocket and drops a handful of quarters into the slot. She ducks her head and blushes; she knows she should know better, but she's always a little surprised when guys drop their money just to look at her. She licks her finger and runs it over her nipple. "So, you like me?"

Yes, he writes. *You seem...friendly.*

She leans back, spreads her pussy lips open for a teasing moment, then lets them close again. "I try," she answers. "So what would you like to talk about?"

You, he writes.

"Sure," she smiles. "What would you like to know?"

He thinks for a moment, then scribbles again. *What part of your body do you like best?*

Her eyebrows shoot up again. "Interesting question. No one's asked me that before."

Really? Nobody?

"Well, nobody in here," she shrugs. "But to answer your question, I'd say...my ass. I like my ass a lot. Would you like to see it?"

He scribbles hastily. *Sure I'd like to see your ass...*

He flips to a new page. *But I want to see your face, too.*

"You got it, bub," she says cheerfully. She leaps to her feet, spins around, flops over at the waist and gapes at him between her legs. "How's this?" she grins.

He laughs and shakes his head. *That's really silly,* he writes.

"You're right," she answers. "I never understood that one either. Okay...let's try this."

She gets on her hands and knees, putting her body in profile. She gives him a smoky look over her shoulder, tousles her hair and growls. Tiger woman, she thinks. Queen of the jungle. She shifts her leg to show him her soft, round ass, arches her back and grinds her hips in slow circles. "How's that?" she asks.

Much better, he writes. *So what do you like doing with your ass, Chloe?*

She doesn't hesitate. "I like to get it fucked," she replies crudely.

Show me.

She puts her finger in her mouth and draws it out slowly, getting it nice and wet. An unexpected shudder goes through her body as she raises her eyes to meet his. His gaze trails down her back like gentle fingers, and she squirms and wriggles, pleased and flattered and oddly bashful. She reaches back with one hand, opens her asscheeks invitingly, and runs her wet finger up and down the crack. He gazes back at her face, solemn and anxious; she gives him a small, coy smile and waits.

Please?

She grins and licks her lips. She wets her finger again, then slowly slides it into her asshole.

A sudden rush of pleasure rolls into her head. She moans and closes her eyes, almost against her will, as she slowly pumps her finger into her ass. A small, tight spot in her throat begins to dissolve, melts down into her breasts and stomach; she bucks her hips up hard, bites her lip, and begins to whimper quietly. Her ass clenches tight around her finger, pulling it in deeper.

She opens her eyes suddenly, remembering where she is, and gives Henry a wild, intent look. His hands are pressed against the glass, clutching the notebook; his eyes are open wide, shining with lechery and delight. She shoves a second finger into her asshole and begins to fuck herself in earnest, hard and crude and a little rough, just the way she likes it. She moans louder, throws her head back, and lets out a sharp little cry of bliss.

She collapses onto the floor, panting dramatically. She rolls onto her back, pulls out her fingers and surreptitiously wipes them onto the grimy carpet. "Oh, my god," she whispers.

He takes a deep breath and pulls away from the glass. *Jesus, you're beautiful,* he writes. *Thank you.*

She props herself up on her elbow. "You're welcome," she says.

Was it real? he writes.

"Mmmmmm," she murmurs. "You bet."

Really?

She hesitates. "Well...yeah," she says uncomfortably. "More or less. I mean, it felt good. Felt real good, actually. But no, I didn't come, if that's what you're asking."

He smiles and nods. *Thanks for being honest,* he writes. *I appreciate that.*

A softer song comes on the jukebox. *So, do you like working here?* Henry writes.

The lie springs to Sheila's lips, the automatic lie hammered into her by months of unspoken training. She gives him a long, serious look, looks around to make sure nobody is listening, and speaks.

"Well...here's the deal," she murmurs, as softly as she can and still have him hear her, as loudly as she can without being overheard.

"Yeah, I do like it. The money's good, and the hours are flexible. I don't have to work forty hours to pay the rent. And the dancing itself is fun. I like to dance and I like my body... and I like sex, I like being sexy." He grins and waggles his eyebrows. "And the other women are amazing. They're smart and funny, and they really take care of each other. I just love them to pieces."

But... he writes.

It all comes out in a rush. "The fucking men," she says bitterly. "They want it all spoon-fed to them. Pussy and pleasure and all the rest of it. They think sex should be like TV, but with hotter babes and no commercials. They just wanna sit back and suck it down like baby birds. They don't smile, they don't say hi, they don't say 'Thank you' or 'You're pretty' or even 'Nice tits, baby.' They just stare like dead fish. Not all of them...but a fuck of a lot of them." She takes a deep breath, startled by her own anger.

He nods. *Men are assholes,* he scribbles.

She laughs heartily, her bitterness broken for the moment. "Thank you," she says. "So...what would you like to see now? Anything special?"

What would you like? he writes.

She chuckles. "Why don't you take your clothes off and dance for me," she jokes. "Just for a change."

He scribbles seriously for a long minute. *Okay. But I'd better warn you, I'm not a very good dancer.*

He sets the pad on the bench, runs his hand through his hair, and slowly begins to undress. She stretches out like a cat and watches in awe, amazed that he took her seriously.

He unbuttons his shirt, slowly, caressing his chest as he uncovers it bit by bit. She plays with her own body in response, moving her hand over her belly as he strips off his shirt and shows her his thin chest. Hesitantly, he begins to roll his torso in slow, snakelike ripples. She can smell herself, the sharp, salty smell her pussy gives off when it wants something really badly. She watches hungrily as he slides his hands down over his hips. He begins to rub his dick through his jeans, and she draws a sudden, ragged breath. Her pulse beats hard inside her clit; she shoves her hand between her thighs and squeezes tight.

Suddenly he stops dancing and snatches up the pad and pen. *I feel silly*, he writes. *I feel like a dork.*

She shakes her head, baffled. "You shouldn't," she replies. "You look great. I'm getting totally wet watching you." She stares meaningfully at his crotch. "Now show me more."

He drops the pad and pen, slumps against the wall, and gives her a moody, smoldering stare like a model for designer jeans. She laughs and nods approvingly. He begins to move again, squirming against the wall. Slowly, teasingly, he unbuckles his belt, unzips his fly, and tugs his swollen dick out of his pants and into the open air. He cradles it in his hand and gives her a wide-open look, proud and fearful and eager for approval.

She ogles his cock and licks her lips, drinking in his eagerness like water. "Very pretty," she says. "Very nice indeed. But I wanna see more. Turn around and pull them all the way down. Show me your ass."

He complies immediately; turns to face the wall and slowly pulls his jeans down over his slim hips. She whistles appreciatively as the fabric drops to his thighs and his bare ass is revealed. He blushes bright red, presses his hands against the wall and bends over to give her a better look. She stares intently at his ass, relishing his exposure, sucking in the view like a starving woman. Her clit thumps hard, demanding attention, and she begins to caress it in earnest. I love a boy who does what I tell him, she thinks.

"Now turn around again," she commands. "Let me see your dick. Let me see you jerk off."

He spins around to face her, jeans around his knees, face flushed, his dick twitching of its own accord. He jams his back against the wall, licks his hand like a dog, and begins to slide it up and down the shaft of his cock.

A sudden flash of longing stabs into her cunt, and she whimpers and spreads her legs wider. She opens her pussy lips with her fingers and thrusts her hips towards the glass, frantically and insistently, forcing her hole into the open, trying to show him as much of herself as she can. His eyes widen as they take in her sopping wet cunt; he grips his cock with a trembling hand as she spreads herself apart and furiously rubs her swollen clit. Their eyes connect; they stare intently, flushed, shivering, mouths hanging open, eyes wide. His hand moves faster and faster; a shudder travels through his body, and he bites his lip, throws his head back, and squirts into his hand. She sees his face contort, and cries out hard, and comes.

They both take a deep breath and slump backwards. Sheila stretches back and clamps her thighs around her hand; Henry collapses against the wall, lost in quiet bliss. At last he pulls his pants up, takes a handkerchief out of his pocket, and wipes the come off his hand. He picks up the pad and pen. *Thank you thank you thank you,* he writes.

"Jesus," she gasps. "You're welcome. Thank you."

That was real...right?

She nods. "Yeah," she answers. "That was real."

The window panel starts to slide down. Henry scrabbles through his pockets and quickly drops another quarter in the slot. The panel slides up again; he spreads his hand and shows her the contents with a sad, wistful smile. One more quarter. He drops it in and shrugs. *How much time do we have?* he writes.

"About a minute," she answers. "Shit. You'd better get dressed."

He pulls his shirt on and zips his pants. *So is your name really Chloe?* he writes.

"No," she replies. "Of course not."

What is it really?

She gives him a long, clear look. Maybe I should make up a fake real name, she thinks. She likes this guy a lot; it'd make him happy to think she'd confided in him. She thinks carefully for a moment, then shakes her head.

"I'm not going to tell you that," she says. "I'm sorry."

Quite all right, he scribbles. *I understand. Thanks for not lying.*

"You're welcome," she replies.

They stare at each other awkwardly, somewhat at a loss for words. "That was wonderful," she says at last. "Really. You made my day."

He kisses his hand and reaches out to touch the glass. The panel drops down, sliding over his hand, clicking shut. "Come back sometime," she calls into the metal plate. She presses her hands against the window, drained and dazed and a bit forlorn, hoping that he heard her.

She feels a light touch on her shoulder. "Hey, Chloe," Tanisha says. "It's time for your break." She gives Sheila a light slap on the rump. "Nice show, girl," she adds. "Hell, you even got me going."

"Thanks," Sheila sighs. "Me, too. Sometimes I really like this job."

"I know what you mean, babe," Tanisha says as Sheila walks off the stage. "I know what you mean."

BENDING

Bending

She loved being bent over. More than any fiddling that might precede it, more than any fumbling sex act that might follow. The moment of being bent over was like a sex act to Dallas, like foreplay and climax blended into one swooning, too-short moment. A hand on her neck, pressing gently but firmly downward, felt like a tongue on her clit; a voice in her ear, telling her calmly and reasonably to bend over and pull down her pants, felt like a cock in her cunt.

She always masturbated in that position. She sometimes masturbated by getting in that position and then doing nothing else. She would stand by the arm of her sofa, by the side of the bed, at the edge of the kitchen table; and she would bare her ass, slowly, and slowly bend herself over... and then she would stand there, bent over, hands on her hips or behind the small of her back, thinking. Thinking about what she looked like, thinking about what she felt like. Thinking about the feel of the air on the skin of her exposed ass. Thinking about hands on her thighs, paddles on her bottom, dicks and dildos in her asshole and her cunt. Thinking about what a dirty hungry girl she was. Thinking, until she came.

The furnishings that crowded Dallas's apartment would be a dead giveaway to anyone who knew what to look for. Sofas and armchairs with wide, firm backs and arms; tables and dressers that were all waist height; a small but varied collection of hairbrushes, vintage and modern. A padded table she had had made for her, its height easily adjustable so her head and torso could be raised or lowered as the mood required. It could pass for a sewing or card table. She called it the bending table. She tried not to use it too often, for fear of using up all the magic.

It was hard sometimes. She saw a video once, where a man bent a woman over a toilet and shoved her head in it while he fucked her in the ass. She thought she would pass out. She watched the scene ten times, pale, wet between her legs, a shaking hand on the remote. She watched it ten times, and then took the video back to the rental place and never watched it again. It made her stomach hurt, the thought that this act had happened—literally, physically, factually happened— to someone who wasn't her.

She did have lovers. Many of them over the years. Dozens if you counted them all, more if you counted very carefully. More than one of these lovers had accused Dallas of being a black hole, an accusation she felt was deeply unfair, not to mention inaccurate. It wasn't that she didn't want to give anything. She simply felt that what she did have to give was sufficient. Her pain, her submission, her ass in the air present-ed like a jewel on a satin pillow, her willingness to do almost anything a person could do in that position... Dallas felt that all of this was a tremendous gift. It wasn't that she didn't want to give anything. It was that she had yet to find a lover who wanted what she had to give. She found this tremendously annoying. Hurtful, too, for sure, and frustrat-ing at times to the point of despair, but mostly just annoying as hell.

And the accusation—"You only like to do one thing"—completely baffled her. It wasn't one thing, she argued to herself on her way home from a particularly frustrating squabble. It wasn't one thing, any more than so-called regular sex was one thing. Being bent over was a whole field of things, an entire genus, with a zillion details that could vary. Wriggling and weeping versus serene submission; being gently guided to the edge of the bed versus being shoved onto the floor; jeans and cotton panties yanked down to her knees versus a flimsy skirt slowly pulled up to reveal her sluttily un-pantied bottom... these were distinct sex acts, obviously and self-evidently, as different as, say, intercourse and oral sex seemed to be for the rest of the world. The portion of the world that she'd been fucking, anyway.

Certain details about her lovers didn't much matter to her. Male, female, neither or both, any of these were fine. Age, race, height, weight, occupation or lack thereof, smoking habits, voting habits, all those things that kept showing up in the personal ads; none of them made much difference to Dallas. Lately, it was beginning to make less and less difference whether she even found them attractive. It was beginning to matter only whether they were willing.

For example.

There was Daria, the photographer. Daria loved seducing people into taking things a little too far, loved getting them to sign the release and then leading them, step by gentle step, from a tasteful, soft-focus nude session into something she'd have to take to Amsterdam to get published. She loved the blush, the not-so-reluctant reluctance, the shame and relief on her subjects' faces at being exposed at last. She was good, and she got what she wanted a lot. And God knows she got good pictures out of Dallas. She got a whole book's worth of pictures out of Dallas, a book she'd have been hard-pressed to get published even in Amsterdam. But she never got the blush. She had Dallas doing things that almost made her own bad self blush, and she talked to Dallas in a low voice about how many people were going to see these pictures and know her dirty secret, and through it all Dallas just smiled, a beatific half-smile like she was gazing on the face of the Holy Virgin. Daria even got out the video camera, a last resort if there ever was one, and she told Dallas about all the filthy leering perverts she was going to sell the tape to on the Internet, and Dallas just spread her asshole wider, and smiled wider. Daria did finally get the photos published, some of them anyway, and she sent Dallas five copies of the book, and Dallas sent back a very sweet thank-you note with an order for ten more copies at the 20 percent discount agreed on in their contract.

There was Jack. That was good for a while. Jack liked a lot of different things, but he was happy to oblige Dallas as long as she was happy to oblige him back. It was pretty damn fun, actually; he knew where she lived, so he could keep her on the hook for hours, groveling on the floor begging for his cock, smacking herself in the pussy and calling herself a cheap whore, bound on her back with his Jockeys in her mouth while he jerked off in her face and told her what a good girl she was. As long as he held out the promise of bending her over and doing things to her from behind, she'd do just about anything for him, and do it with a song in her heart. But he knew her heart wasn't in it. He knew that all she really wanted was the bending-over part, and someone who craved it as much as she did. And he didn't. It was perfectly fine, but he didn't have that sort of dedication to the one fetish. His fetish was variety. And ultimately, what he wanted was someone who wanted him, someone desperate for his particular cock, his Jockeys in their mouth, someone who wasn't just lending him their mouth as a trade-off for his hands on their ass. So the two of them broke it off. They were still friends, though, and they still did it sometimes, when her ads were running dry and his boyfriend had other plans.

There was B.J., a butch top who'd call herself that to anyone who would listen. She loved having cute girls bend over for her, loved to beat them until they cried prettily and begged her to stop. But Dallas never would. Oh, she'd cry alright; she'd cry and whimper, scream and wriggle, yank frantically against her ropes or beat her fists on the bed. But she never asked B.J. to stop. Not once. B.J. would beat her until the welts ran together; but when she dropped the belt and sneered, "Had enough?" Dallas would inevitably draw a breath and say, "No, sir. I can take more." Like it was a fucking gift or something. B.J. didn't think it was a fucking gift. She thought it was a challenge, or a mockery even. The last time Dallas said it, B.J. shrugged in disgust, tossed her paddle into her bag, and said "Fine. You win." She picked up her bag and her motorcycle jacket without another word, while Dallas stayed in position, bent over with one foot on the floor and the other splayed out on the bed, looking over her shoulder with a puzzled expression. B.J. gave Dallas one last withering look and slammed out the front door—and hovered in the hallway, waiting for Dallas to run out and call after her. She stayed long enough to hear Dallas make herself come, quickly and loudly. She didn't stay long enough to hear Dallas pick up the phone and call Jack for a lengthy gripe-fest about asshole tricks who thought sex was a competition.

There was Jeffrey—Jeff, Jeffrey, he didn't care—who met her through her ad online. He couldn't believe his luck; they'd been talking in the coffee shop for maybe five minutes when she looked him up and down and said calmly, "So if I take you back to my place now, will you bend me over and fuck me in the ass?" At first he thought it was a scam, thought her boyfriend would jump out from behind her door and mug him or something; but she sighed impatiently and said, "Fine. Your place, my place. A motel. Whatever," and he dropped a twenty on the coffee shop table and took her to a motel down the block. And then he really couldn't believe his luck. The door shut behind them, and she tossed her purse in the corner, jerked up her skirt, flopped over the dresser, spread her ass cheeks apart with her hands, and started begging him to stick it in. She didn't have to beg him twice. He scrambled out of his pants, shoved a condom onto his dick, and hastily guided himself into her open, gentle asshole. He fucked her slow and sweet until she squirmed and bucked and whimpered for him to fuck her hard and fast, and then he slammed her, five or six good slams before he came. But then she started getting weird on him. She stayed bent over the dresser even after he pulled out, and she started talking about him putting things into her ass. She had some things in her purse, she said. When he went silent she started sweet-talking, saying they could do it anywhere he wanted, on the floor, against the wall, in the bathroom over the toilet seat. Her voice trembled a bit when she mentioned the toilet seat. When he stayed silent, she looked abashed, said she knew she was hard to deal with sometimes, said she could see why he might be angry, said if he felt like he had to punish her she'd understand. At which point he remembered an urgent appointment, scrambled back into his pants, and made the most graceful thirty-second exit he could muster. He wasn't sure, but he thought he saw her reaching for her purse as he closed the door.

There was Betsy.

Betsy saw Dallas's ad on the Net. She liked how direct it was, blunt, stripped down to the firm core of the advertiser's need. (This was after months of ad-writing trial and error, but Betsy didn't know that at the time.) The ad read simply, "I want you to bend me over and do things to me from behind. I don't want to do anything else. If you want to do that too, let's talk."

Betsy wanted to do that, too. They talked.

"Do you like bending over?" Betsy asked. "Or do you like being bent over? These distinctions are important." It was a weekday afternoon, and the café was empty except for a somber-looking student with a stack of physics books and the pink-haired girl behind the counter.

Dallas considered the question. "Both," she replied. "Mostly the second. But both are good."

"Over furniture? Over the knee? Hands and knees?"

"Yes," Dallas replied. Betsy waited, but Dallas seemed to think she'd answered the question, so Betsy went on. "Is there anything you particularly like having done to you once you're bent over?"

Dallas laughed and blushed, at herself and at the absurdity of the question. "Oh, one or two things. How much time have you got?"

"Give me the Cliff Notes version," Betsy smiled. "We can go over details later."

"The Cliff Notes. Well. Pain. Fucking, ass and cunt. Submission. Humiliation. Exhibition. Violation. Power and control stuff. Ummm... I think that's most of it. I'm sure I'm missing something—"

"Okay, I get the picture," Betsy said. "What about punishment? Did you forget punishment?"

"Well," Dallas said. "Punishment. Well, sure, punishment is fine. But you asked what I 'specially liked, and that's not really on the list. It's..." She grinned. "It's just a little hard to make myself buy it. No matter how much it hurts. If I'm bent over and getting done, it's kind of hard to convince myself that I'm there because I've done something wrong. But if you want to punish me, if that's something you really like, I can get into it. Do you?"

"I do," Betsy answered. "It's not, like, the only thing, but at least sometimes. So what about—is there anything you don't like having done to you once you're bent over?"

Dallas smiled. Mona Lisa with a canary in her mouth. "Not that I've found yet."

She thought for a moment and went on, a bit more human. "I mean. Of course there are things I don't like. But it... I know this sounds like it doesn't make sense, but I like things that I don't like. Being made to do things I don't like. The more I don't like it, sometimes, the better it is. It feels more..."

She trailed off, dissatisfied with her explanation. But Betsy was nodding before Dallas had finished. "Yes. What you said. It definitely feels—more."

They both drifted off into private reverie, Betsy contemplating her tea and a smudge on the table, Dallas gazing at a parking meter just outside the café window. Betsy pulled out first. "Limits?" she asked.

"The usual, I guess. No scars, no trips to the hospital. Nothing permanent. Let's see... no animals or kids. Nothing in public that could get us thrown in jail. I strongly prefer no shit play or Nazi stuff, but if that's crucial to you, I'll deal."

"The usual."

"Yeah. You know, the stuff most people don't like." Dallas paused. "Does that sound okay?"

Betsy nodded judiciously, trying to play it cool. "Sure. That sounds okay."

"Just okay?" Dallas asked with a flutter of her lashes, and Betsy gave up and cracked a grin. "Okay, fine," she replied. "It sounds more than okay. It sounds like I've found the Lost City of Gold. Where the hell did you come from, anyway?"

Dallas smiled, more canary than Mona Lisa this time. "Thanks."

They both paused, eyes linked, awkward. "So," Betsy said. "Yes or no? Or maybe?"

"Yes."

Betsy refrained from pumping her fist in victory. "Now, or later?"

Dallas smiled wider. "Yes."

So they had their idyllic interlude. All of it in soft focus, lit with an amber light at a flattering angle, with music by Burt Bacharach playing in the background.

They played teacher and student, Betsy in glasses and a dark grey dress, Dallas in navy blue knee socks and a plaid skirt, standing and pouting while Betsy scolded her for inattention and poor study habits. The first time they played, the first time Betsy instructed her to bend over and pull down her panties, Dallas felt a hard thump in her clit, and she had to think hard and remind herself about the game to keep from grinning. She bent over the makeshift desk and pulled her white panties down to her thighs, slowly, making a show of shyness and reluctance. The words "bending over and pulling down my panties" rolled through her mind like the sound of a river. She savored the words, the moment, the image of the scene that she had in her mind, while Betsy smacked her bottom with a thick wooden ruler and made her recite the multiplication tables. When Dallas made a mistake, Betsy got out the metal ruler—one stroke, hard, for each mistake she had made so far— then returned to the wooden ruler for a steady, rhythmic smacking, while Dallas sniffled and started over from the beginning. Dallas liked this game—the fifth time they played it as much as the first, although in a different way. She loved how easy it was to make it go on. All she had to do was forget what nine times eight was.

They played doctor and patient, Betsy in a white lab coat she'd picked up at a yard sale, Dallas in her most respectable street clothes. She felt so dirty doing it in her street clothes. She loved her slut gear, of course, but there was something about being bent over the exam table in a cotton-poly skirt-suit and a pair of drugstore pantyhose. She could almost believe that she was a normal person, could almost feel a twinge of embarrassment at Betsy's elaborate exam techniques. She felt genuinely unnerved, almost, when Betsy inserted a cold and wet rectal thermometer, or slid in a well-lubed anal speculum and slowly cranked it open to "get a better look," or told her to undress completely from the waist down and kneel over the basin to receive an enema. She could just about feel the shame and smallness, the dignity stripped, the confidence in the doctor's professionalism gradually fading into uncertainty and a vague sense that something was wrong. And Betsy came up with the best excuses for the more excessive of her outrages. Experimental equipment, nerve and reflex testing, a serious medical condition that required radical treatment; any of these could justify storing steel probes in a jar of ice water, or pinching Dallas's thighs with a pair of forceps while making her count to a thousand by sevens, or inserting a metal egg in her vagina and swiping her clitoris from behind with a slender fiberglass rod. Betsy loved this game, and was good at it. She never stretched disbelief to the breaking point, never played doctor in spike-heeled boots or put a ball gag in the patient's mouth. She sometimes adjusted her trousers a bit too vigorously, or pulled her lab coat down tight against her nipples, but nothing that Dallas would notice with her back turned. Which, of course, it always was.

They played uncle and little girl. Betsy couldn't handle playing daddy, but she could be the uncle just fine. Sometimes she'd be a good uncle—well, comparatively good, anyway—taking Dallas over her knee for a good, simple, bare-bottomed spanking, a punishment for some childish misdeed. And sometimes she'd be a bad uncle, fondling the bare-bottomed girl after her spanking, caressing her pinkened skin, sneaking a snakey finger between her legs, telling her to be a good girl and do what Uncle said... and getting angry when Dallas started to cry, and spanking her some more. Spanking her harder. Punishing her for crying, and fiddling between her legs while she spanked her even more. That was a good game. They played that one a lot.

They played rapist and victim, in an alley in the middle of nowhere near where Betsy worked. They arranged a time, and Betsy got there late, late enough to get Dallas anxious and pacing, jumpy, jumping out of her skin at the sudden hand over her mouth and the knife at her throat. "Shut up, cunt," Betsy murmured, as she grabbed Dallas by the hair and wrestled her to the cement wall. "Lean against it. Bend over. Now." Dallas complied, shaking, pressing her hands to the rough wall, as Betsy yanked her skirt up and sliced open the crotch of her panties. She kicked Dallas's legs apart; Dallas stumbled, and Betsy's knife was at her throat again, the other hand groping between Dallas's legs. "Stick your ass out, cunt," Betsy snarled, and Dallas obeyed, disoriented, in a well-trained response to her lover's instructions, in terrified compliance with the knife and the rough hands. She started to cry as she felt Betsy fumble with her fly, felt Betsy's dick pressing clumsily against her pussy, felt her hole being pushed open, filled up. She felt Betsy's hips tremble between her thighs, felt the stupid anger in her voice as she let out a stream of crude, repetitive cursing. "Keep your ass stuck out, cunt, bitch, fucking cunthole, I'm sticking it in you, sticking it, fucking you, fuck you all I want, fucking bitch, cunt, fucking your cunt, spread it, spread your hole, your fucking hole, fuckhole, fuckhole, cunt..." Dallas kept crying, kept bending over, kept spreading her legs apart and sticking her ass out, as Betsy used her cunt and came inside her, hard, jerking. They agreed afterwards that it had been a good game, but not one you could play very often. Betsy even meant it, almost.

And sometimes they just played. They played "make Dallas crawl on the floor with a buttplug in her ass and another one in her mouth." Or "tie Dallas down to the bending table and fuck her mouth with a strap-on dildo." Or "make Dallas touch her toes a hundred times and smack her on the ass each time." Or even just "bend Dallas over the bed and fuck her from behind."

It was, as they say, all good.

"So is there anything you want?" Betsy asked. They were lying sprawled in Betsy's rumpled bed, in a nest of dildos and lube bottles, piled-up pillows and dirty magazines. Dallas was idly playing with the inside of Betsy's thigh.

"You mean a specific thing we haven't done yet?" Dallas replied. "Well... there's this thing I saw in a video once, a scene in a bathroom, this guy bends a girl over the toilet and dunks her head into it while he—"

"Oh yes." Betsy nodded vigorously. "Yes. I've seen that video. Definitely. Anytime. But that's not exactly... I mean, is there anything you want? Bigger than that." She took Dallas's hand and held it on her belly. "Sometimes you seem, not unhappy, but... restless. Like there's something you've forgotten. Is there something you want? Other than just the next scene?"

Dallas pondered. "Maybe," she said. "Can I think about it?"

She thought about it. Thought about it all that night, and the next morning. Thought about it on the bus to work, on her coffee break, her lunch break, her second coffee break. Thought about it on the bus ride home. Thought about it the next day, and the next, and the one after that.

What did she want?

It wasn't a scene. She could think of scenes from here to Texas and back without breaking a sweat. Scenes weren't hard to think of. But Betsy was right, there was something she wanted that was bigger than a scene. Something she'd never quite gotten from a scene, not even the good ones, not even the amazing ones. Even the scenes that left her blind and gasping, also left her... she didn't know what. She spent the better part of an afternoon doing some tedious filing and thinking about what, exactly. Not unhappy, not dissatisfied, but...

Unfinished. That was it. It dawned on her on the bus ride home. She felt unfinished. Hungry still. Like she'd had a huge meal, with chicken and potatoes and two slices of pie, and was still staring at the pie thinking that a third slice might be nice. And for all her sex-positive, slut-positive, I-am-woman-watch-me-fuck attitude, she still thought her hosts would think she was greedy if she asked for that third piece of pie. And not without reason. Some of her hosts had thought she was greedy for wanting the first one.

But Betsy was different. She knew Betsy wanted her to have all the pie she wanted. She knew Betsy would happily bake her an entire pie, and feed it to her with a silver fork on bone china, and then bake her another if she was still hungry for more. And she knew Betsy would get off on it. She knew her lust was safe.

The next time she saw Betsy, she kissed her hello and said, "Yes. There is."

"I'm sorry, babyface," Betsy said. "Non-sequitur alert. What?"

"Your question," Dallas answered, rolling her eyes. "The one you asked me the last time you saw me." She settled into her seat, told the waiter that she wanted water now and a glass of the house red with dinner, folded her hands on the table, and said, "This is it. I want to do it until I'm done. I want you to bend me over and do me, until I'm ready to stop."

"Okay," Betsy said. "Sure. Why not?"

Dallas shook her head. "No. I mean it. Until I'm done. Like, done done. I mean... don't take this the wrong way, most of the time when we stop I'm fine, we always stop at a good place. But I could also keep going. I want you to bend me over and do me until that isn't true. I want to keep doing it until I really, really, don't want to do it anymore. Can't do it anymore. I want to feel... like, even for just a few hours... like I've had enough."

"Wow," Betsy said. "Okay. Sure. Should we set aside a weekend?"

"No," Dallas said. "We should set aside a week."

Betsy looked at Dallas. "Oh," she said. "Oh. Give me a minute."

Dallas nodded and got up to use the bathroom, rinsing her face and fixing her lipstick and generally killing time. Betsy continued to scowl at the spot on the table, her chin in her hand. She was still staring when Dallas came back. Finally she spoke. "No."

Dallas's face fell. "No?"

"No. We should set aside two weeks. One won't be enough. We'll feel rushed. I want to do this right."

"What if it we're not done in two weeks?" Dallas asked. It was Friday evening, and Betsy had met her after work, their last day of work before their vacation.

"We'll quit our jobs," Betsy replied. Dallas wasn't sure if she was kidding.

And so they had their second interlude.

Day One:

"Starting now, all you are is your body," Betsy said as she bent Dallas over the bending table and inserted a medium-size buttplug. It was Saturday, late morning. They had woken and showered about twenty minutes earlier. "Just your body, from your waist to your knees. Your ass, and your pussy, and your thighs. You're here for me to use when I feel like it; when I don't feel like it, you're still here. You're like the vibrator in the drawer, or a porno video. Get used to it."

She laid her hand between Dallas's shoulder blades, held it there for a moment, then let go. "If you have to stretch, or eat or drink, or use the bathroom, you can get up and do it, but I want you back here as soon as you're done. If your legs and back need a break, you can lie facedown on the bed for a while, but come back to the table as soon as you can." She drew her fingers across Dallas's lips like she was sealing a Ziploc bag. "Don't ask me for permission, just do it. I'm not going to gag you, so I'll trust you to gag yourself. I don't want to hear your voice. Your voice isn't relevant. Your voice doesn't exist. Until I speak to you again." She took a cloth out of a drawer and draped it over the back of Dallas's head. "Now stay."

Betsy patted Dallas on the behind and left her there while she puttered around the apartment: watching TV, reading magazines, surfing the Web. Every now and then she'd go over to Dallas, take the buttplug out, and put things in her asshole: toys, fingers, dildos of various sizes. Casually, without much in the way of intent; no sweet slow seduction, no pounding toward the finish line. Just things in her ass, there, and then not there. For five minutes, or ten, or thirty... poking and prodding and swirling around, then removed and the buttplug replaced, and then Dallas would be left by herself over the bending table. Or Betsy would keep the buttplug in and put things in Dallas's cunt. Toys, fingers. She'd stick in her strap-on and hold it still, press it inside Dallas's pussy for a bit, and then remove it. None of it was at a slow pace; it generally happened slowly, but in the strictest sense it wasn't a pace at all. It wasn't really fucking. It was penetration. And then it would end, as abruptly as it started, and Betsy would be gone from the room.

As the mood struck her, Betsy would go to Dallas and do things; as the mood passed, she'd wander off. Dallas could smell her own breath under the cloth, could feel a light breeze stirring her naked skin. She could hear the TV in the other room, and Betsy laughing and popping open a soda. Then Betsy would return, and there would be more things in her pussy, or her asshole. Every half hour, or ten minutes, or hour. Dallas wasn't sure anymore. She was beginning to lose track of time. The windows were shut, the drapes pulled tight. She took a pee break and glanced at the clock in the bathroom. Betsy had taken it down.

The cloth over her head and shoulders made Dallas intensely conscious of her ass. Not that she wasn't always conscious of her ass, but having her vision gone made it easier to picture what she looked like, the cloth not just hiding her head but putting the bottom half of her body in the spotlight. Like a diamond ring in one of those boxes, the jewel framed and displayed in velvet, the ring itself buried underneath, functional but not very interesting. She couldn't help but be turned on. She was naked and bent over and her lover was in the next room planning God knows what, so getting turned on was almost inevitable. But her arousal was frustrating. Nothing was being done about it. She was beginning to get that maybe nothing would be done about it. This was about getting Betsy off: her own desire, like her voice, was irrelevant. Only her body mattered, from her belly to her knees. And when Betsy was leaving her alone, like she was doing now, like she had done for a while now, her skin tingled, impatient, hungry, sad. Her mind started drifting away from her head and down below her belly, paying meticulous attention to her ass and her pussy and her thighs, which were getting antsy and edging toward frantic in their demands for attention.

She came back to earth for a minute as her knees started demanding attention as well, and she lay facedown on the bed, the cloth draped over her head, to give herself a break. Except that it wasn't a break. Betsy came in and started fiddling with her clit from behind, spreading Dallas's thighs apart, holding her lips open with one hand while she fingered her with the other. Dallas sighed with relief and pathetic gratitude as her mind raced back into her brain and her pussy gobbled up the sensation like it was starving. The relief and gratitude didn't last. Within a minute, she was gritting her teeth and balling her hands into angry fists, as Betsy twiddled idly with her clit like she was twanging a jaw harp, steady and unchanging, too fast and hard for Dallas to ignore, too soft and slow for her to come. Dallas pressed her face into the mattress and ground her teeth so she wouldn't whimper out loud, and Betsy took Dallas's pussy lips in her fingers and spread them apart, studying her, like she was checking the turkey to see if it was done. She examined Dallas's clit for a minute or so, then left the room to watch the rest of the ball game. Dallas squeezed her eyes shut tight and her pussy tighter, clenched her anus around the buttplug, then steadied herself and walked back to the bending table. I am a vibrator in a drawer, she said to herself. I am a porno video. I don't want anything. She bent over the table and tried to make herself believe it.

She was repeating these words like a mantra when the pain started. Betsy was apparently getting bored, and instead of sticking her fingers into Dallas's pussy on her way to the kitchen, now she'd slap Dallas's ass. Or she'd stop for a few moments and beat it with a spatula, or a ruler, or something hastily grabbed out of the toy chest. No buildup, and no cooldown, just a hard stroke, or a series of hard strokes, on the way to somewhere else. Dallas had no idea what was next, or when, or if. It could be the smack of a hairbrush, wide and flat, landing again and again. Five minutes later it could be the crop, whistling out of nowhere, lashing into her thigh once and then disappearing. Half an hour later it could be the open hand. Or fingers, pinching, mean little pinches on the sorest spots. It might get mixed up with other stuff, a finger tickling her clit while a hairbrush struck her on one thigh, or a few strokes with the strap-on between blows of the belt. Or it wouldn't, it would be pure, free of distraction. There would be pain, or penetration, or fondling, and then not. Just nothing. Just an empty pussy, and a filled-up asshole, and a naked ass. Dallas began to lose track of things other than time.

When Betsy finally spoke, Dallas jumped. "Okay," Betsy said. "I think we're done with that for now. You should stand up and stretch, move around a little, before we move on." She took the cloth off of Dallas's head, and Dallas creaked up and looked around. Betsy had turned the light on. It was dusk.

That night, they watched *Star Trek* while they ate like they always did. Dallas lay on her belly on the floor and ate from a tray, the nightgown Betsy had put on her pulled up around her waist. Betsy sat on the sofa. After dinner, she had Dallas lie across her lap, and gave her a long, gentle spanking, soft tapping slaps, almost a massage, while they watched a movie on TV. She slipped a vibrator onto her lap just under Dallas's hips, and Dallas rubbed against it frantically, and came, and came, and came.

They went to bed early that night. Dallas curled up on her side to drift off, and Betsy shook her. "No," she said. "I want you to sleep on your front."

Dallas stared at her, confused. "Huh?"

"I want you to sleep on your front," Betsy repeated. "I want your ass in the air, even when you're asleep. If I wake up in the night and want a fondle or a dry hump, I'm going to want it right away." She pressed Dallas's shoulder down. "So turn over."

Dallas flipped onto her belly. The skin of her ass was still sore and tingly, her asshole was still open and tender, and she was very conscious of the feel of it as she burrowed her face into the pillow. She went to sleep almost immediately; she slept solid, dreamed a strange dream, turned onto her side in her sleep. Betsy climbed out of bed at once. She removed the cane from the closet, shook Dallas awake, and pressed her onto her belly. "You get one now," she said calmly. "If you do it again, you'll get two. A third time..."

Still half drowsy, Dallas felt the cane lash onto her bewildered ass, like a tree branch in a nighttime storm. She screamed politely into her pillow and didn't complain, but when it was over, she looked over her shoulder with hurt and puzzlement and something that wasn't quite tears, and Betsy relented. "Look," she explained. "I'm not mad. I'm not punishing you. I know you can't control what you do when you're asleep. I'm just... training you. You wanted to be bent over or facedown all the time, and I'm training your body to do that." She smiled, a lizard smile, unrelenting again. "And I'm giving myself a hard-on. It gives me a hard-on to wake up in the night and see your ass in the air, and it gives me a hard-on to beat you if it's not. So deal. This is what you wanted. If you don't want it—"

Dallas sniffled, and nodded, and burrowed her face into the pillow to get back to sleep. She woke one more time to feel Betsy sigh and get out of bed; she immediately flipped over and buried her face in the pillow. She raised her ass a few inches, screamed two muffled screams, and then nodded quietly and shivered herself to sleep.

Day Two:

Dallas slept late that morning, and Betsy was already up and dressed when she woke. "Morning, cupcake," Betsy said. "You up?" Dallas nodded sleepily. "Okay, then," Betsy said. "Let's go."

She started rummaging in Dallas's closet, pulling out an assortment of outfits and laying them out on the bed. "Let's start with this," she said, and handed Dallas the flippy black skirt, the black lace panties, and the push-up bra. Dallas dressed in a hurry, and stood still while Betsy looked her up and down. "Lovely," Betsy said. "Damn."

She led Dallas to the end of the blue sofa. "Let's start here," she said. She pressed Dallas between her shoulder blades, bending her over the sofa's wide, generously padded arm. This was one of Dallas's favorite places; it felt impetuous and slutty, and at the same time completely comfortable. She pressed against the upholstery with a sweet familiarity. Betsy took her time, pressing her down slowly with one hand while she pulled up Dallas's skirt and pulled down her panties with the other. She held Dallas there for a long moment. Then she spoke. "Alright. Now straighten up and cover yourself."

Dallas flinched, startled and disappointed. What the hell, she thought. That was such a good beginning. Did I do something wrong? Where is she going with this? She hitched up her panties and let her skirt fall back down, staring at the floor with a puzzled frown. Betsy took her hand, gave a reassuring squeeze, and led her over to her kitchen table. She suddenly squeezed harder, twisted Dallas's arm behind her back, and gave her a hard shove, snapping her over the table. She jerked Dallas's skirt up and her panties down, then grabbed her other arm, pinning them both behind her back. Dallas sighed, and struggled against Betsy's grip, trying to arch her back and raise her ass in the air.

Betsy dug her fingers in and pressed down harder, tightening the grip on Dallas's wrists and pressing them into the small of her back. Then she let go, suddenly. "Pull up your pants, and stand up," she said.

Dallas complied, more confused than before. She followed, bewildered, as Betsy led her back into the living room and stood her in front of the leather armchair. "Kneel in front of it," she said. "Bend over it. Pull your skirt up and your panties down, and then rest your hands on the cushion."

Dallas smiled. She was starting to get it. The moment of being bent over, the few seconds in which she moved from standing tall to lowering her head and offering her ass, those few seconds felt like the Assumption of Mary into Heaven. And they never lasted long enough. As passionate as she was about the position of being bent over, and all the things that could be done to her there, her obsession with the act of being bent over was even more overwhelming. And she had never once gotten enough of it. But now Betsy was going to give her that moment, over and over again. Dallas knelt in front of the armchair, submissive, grateful, and very slowly began to bend over into the seat. She pressed her breasts into the leather and began to pull up her skirt, sliding the hem of the silky material over her thighs and slowly up to her waist, vividly aware of how she looked. She knew that the contours of her bottom were visible through her lace panties, temptingly revealed and at the same time coyly concealed. She stretched and arched, and felt her flesh swell against the thin fabric. She hitched her thumbs into the waistband of her panties and began to slide them down, paying careful attention to every inch of skin she exposed to her lover. When she had pulled her panties all the way down to her thighs, she placed her hands on the cushion, rested her face between them, and waited peacefully.

Betsy watched her quietly for a moment, then spoke. "Okay. Get up. Let's try a costume change. The hot pants, I think."

Betsy didn't even bother pulling Dallas's hot pants down. She just bent her over the back of the faded maroon love seat, then made her stand up and do it again, watching the curve of her cheeks bulge out from the bottom of the cheap shiny fabric. She made Dallas stand up and do it again, this time kneeling on the floor to bend over the coffee table. Then another costume change: she put Dallas in the plaid skirt and knee socks, and bent her over the computer table, stern and severe. Then over the ottoman, sweet and nasty. Over the blue sofa again, this time in a long full skirt and no panties, with a good five minutes to pull the skirt all the way up. Dallas was getting dizzy. The slow rhythm of being bent over and straightened up, bent over and straightened up, made her feel like she was getting fucked; but instead of each stroke lasting a few seconds, each of these strokes lasted a minute or more, and the whole thing was taking hours. She felt like she was being fucked, not in her cunt or her ass, but in her brain, and in her bones and muscles. Betsy raised the bending table up to its highest height and bent Dallas over it, her jeans and cotton panties pulled down to her ankles. She made Dallas get up, lowered the table an inch, and did it all again. Another inch, and then again. And again, until Dallas had been bent over her beloved table at every possible angle. Dallas was weak with gratitude.

When the table was at its lowest point, Betsy held Dallas over it for a long minute, letting Dallas linger on her precious magic object, letting her feel it at its most humbling angle. She then pulled her up abruptly and dressed her in a tight black ultra-short minidress, white lace panties, and black pumps. She dug a large handbag out of Dallas's closet, and started filling it with junk: lipsticks, compacts, condoms, keys to old apartments, loads and loads of loose change. She zipped it shut and handed it to Dallas.

"We're taking this show on the road," she said. "We're going to the mall. When we're there, I'm going to give you a signal, and you're going to drop this handbag and bend over to pick it up. You're going to keep your legs straight and bend at the waist, unless I tell you otherwise. You're going to do it as slowly as you can without it looking suspicious, and you're going to straighten up slowly. And you're going to do it as many times as I tell you."

Dallas's stomach dropped through her shoes. Her wobbly-kneed gratitude blew away like a candy wrapper, rapidly replaced by stubbornness and fear. She did not want to do this. She not want to do this. As much as she loved giving it up, she was something of a control freak about it, and this felt out of control, the real and scary kind, not a rollercoaster but a car wreck.

She shook her head firmly. "I don't want to," she said.

"I know," Betsy replied. "Let's go."

"Please. No. I really, really, do not want to do this."

"I hear you," Betsy said. "You really do not want to do this. Now let's get going. You can take a minute if you want, but unless you're calling your safeword, let's go."

Dallas was silent on the short drive to the mall. She was alarmed to the point of passivity, and disappointed and pissed in the bargain. Just a few minutes ago she had been relaxed and high and totally sunk into her body, and now she was clenching her fingers and grinding her teeth. She looked over at Betsy, who was driving calmly if a bit too quickly, smirking at the road like it was telling her a dirty joke. It occurred to Dallas that Betsy was getting off on her discomfort, and she hunched her shoulders and glared out the window in dramatic despair.

Betsy patted her knee. "Remember our first date, honey?" she asked.

Dallas nodded, and continued to glower out the window.

"Remember that thing you said, about liking to do things you don't like?"

Dallas looked at Betsy suspiciously, and nodded again.

"So quit sulking," Betsy said. "Get into it. Submit to my all-powerful will, or something. Revel in the depths to which you will sink to satisfy my debauched whims. And do it fast. We're here."

Dallas lowered her eyes and nodded. Her irritation ebbed off a bit, leaving room for a clean, simple fear. They pulled into the parking lot, and Betsy kissed Dallas's hand. "You're on," she said.

They walked into the mall, Dallas willing herself to put one foot in front of the other, stiff and self-conscious, her gaze darting around her and then returning to Betsy's hands. They wandered for a bit, Betsy giving Dallas time to adjust and settle in, or perhaps giving her time to get even more wound up. They were in front of the shoe store when Betsy gave her signal, a discreet hand gesture, and stepped back a few feet. Dallas closed her eyes, and dropped her handbag.

She was completely conscious of her body. She knew how her calves looked in the black pumps, how her thighs looked disappearing up into the short black dress. She hung on to this anxious self-awareness, used it to remember Betsy's precise instructions and force herself into them. She kept her legs stiff, arched her back as she bent over like she was at a yoga class. She could feel her tight dress riding up. She knew that her panties were peeping out from under the hem, the curves and shadows of the bottom of her ass clearly visible through the white lace. She picked up the handbag and stood up slowly, keeping her back arched on the way back up, waiting until she was upright to pull at the hem of her dress. It was over in less than a minute.

She took a deep breath. That wasn't so bad. She was still here, still breathing. She looked around anxiously; she thought she saw a couple of guys hastily look away, but she couldn't be sure.

Betsy strolled over to her and guided her down the promenade. "That was delightful," she whispered in her ear. "A lovely beginning." She stopped in front of the record store, stepped back, and gave the signal again.

The second time was a little easier for Dallas. The third time a little easier still, and the fourth. Her body was falling into its new habit, obeying her a bit more smoothly. And it was also getting harder each time. As her body relaxed, she could feel what it was feeling more clearly, and she was increasingly conscious of where she was, and who, and why. She was exposing herself to the world, inviting complete strangers to look at her ass and see her true nature, and it was for real, not a masturbation fantasy, not a game at a sex party. It was excruciating... and it was why she was here, not just here in the mall, but here in the world. Each time she bent over, each time she forced herself to ignore her instincts and obey her lover, she felt a warm rush swelling high inside her belly. She dropped her purse again at Betsy's signal, and let the resistance and humiliation engulf her.

It was just getting easier for Betsy. Betsy stayed alert and self-contained, keeping her breath even and her hands in her pockets. She repeated her signal every five or ten minutes, sometimes watching Dallas as her skirt rode up over her panties, sometimes watching the shoppers as they stared at her girl. She thought that mall security might be onto them when she kept seeing the same guard over again, but when she saw the glassy look in his eyes and his gaze hovering around Dallas's midsection, she stopped worrying about it. She could see Dallas blush as she bent over in front of the pretzel stand, and felt her own pussy tighten in her jeans. She strode over to Dallas and took her by the arm.

"Now unzip your purse," Betsy commanded. "Dig around in it, fix your lipstick or something. Don't zip it again." Dallas complied, puzzled, and Betsy continued. "The next time I signal you, drop the purse. Be sure to drop it upside down, so the stuff gets scattered all over the floor. Then get on your hands and knees to pick it up. Keep your knees apart, and keep your back arched, and wiggle your hips as you crawl. And take your time. I want you on the floor for a good two minutes at least."

Dallas stared at her in dismay and disbelief. She started to speak, saw the resolve and the greed on Betsy's face, and closed her mouth. Her dismay deepened when Betsy stopped in front of the busy sports bar, stepped back several yards, and gave the signal.

Dallas took a deep breath, and upended her handbag onto the floor. She saw the keys and condoms scatter a good twenty feet away, and cringed, and dropped to her hands and knees. She tried to block out the mall, the bar, the sound of footsteps and the fountain, but blocking out the world just made her that much more conscious of herself, her body. She could feel her dress riding up as she crawled and squirmed, not just showing a tantalizing glimpse of her panties and the bottom of her butt, but slowly riding up over her hips. She desperately wanted to yank it down, to snap her legs together, to give herself some reprieve from the free show she was giving. She could feel the hem of her dress inching up over the curve of her ass, her cheeks pressing into the lace, and she knew that her ass was on display, not naked but as good as naked, in some ways better than naked. Her pussy was wet, and the panties were thin, and she was convinced that the dampness was showing through. She felt that if she pulled her dress up to her waist and her panties down to her knees, she couldn't be offering a clearer invitation. She could see the shoppers and the barflies out of the corner of her eye as she crawled, some glancing at her and then jerking their gaze away in embarrassment, some glancing away and then peeking back surreptitiously, some staring as openly as they could get away with, eyes wide open, disbelieving in their luck. She looked up at Betsy, and saw her face, greedy, breathing hard. She could see that Betsy wasn't done yet. She deliberately knocked the condoms across the floor; she scrabbled after them, and saw Betsy shudder.

Dallas was still on her hands and knees when Betsy raced over to her and helped her up. "Let's go," Betsy said, oblivious to the furtive crowd that had gathered, or maybe just not caring what they thought. She grabbed Dallas by the elbow, hastily led her out of the mall, and drove them back to Dallas's place like a bat out of hell. She slammed the door shut behind them and shoved Dallas forward onto the hallway floor; Dallas was practiced in catching a fall by now, and she scrambled into position, knees and face on the floor, back arched, thighs spread. Betsy dropped her keys and lunged. She grabbed Dallas's pussy and began mauling her, pinching her clit, grabbing her lips in a handful and squeezing like a vise, shoving her fingers inside her sopping hole for a few quick jabs and then smearing her juices onto her lips. They both came within minutes, Dallas whimpering and licking the floor, Betsy jabbering an incoherent stream of dirty talk.

That night Dallas awoke with a jerk, thinking she'd turned over onto her side again. Startled and sleepy, she realized that she was on her belly and that Betsy was caressing her ass. "Go back to sleep if you like," Betsy said. "I'm just going to use you for a minute here." Dallas lay still, half asleep, as Betsy straddled her ass and started idly masturbating. Dallas pushed her ass up to reach her lover, but Betsy shook her head and pressed her hand into the small of Dallas's back. "Stay put," she said. Dallas was wide awake by now, but she held very still, stifling her moans and keeping her squirming in check, as Betsy ground her pussy into Dallas's ass, and fingered her own clit, and made herself come.

Day Three:

Dallas slept like a rock that night, a rock with strange, intense dreams. Betsy shook her awake, much earlier than Dallas was ready for, and led her, sleepy and protesting, to the shower. "In," she said. "Elbows and knees. Face away from the faucet." Dallas complied. She was still groggy, and the blast of warm water did little to wake her up. Betsy's soapy hands on her body were soothing, the shower massager was comforting and familiar even as Betsy directed it away from her torso and focused it between her legs. Dallas had dreamed about sex all night, dreamed that she was bending over the toilet at her office and masturbating, dreamed that her ass was being spread open by invisible hands and fucked by an invisible cock, and now she had a soapy hand on her breasts and a steady thrumming of water on her clit and her asshole. It didn't seem all that different. She noticed Betsy eyeing her watch, filed it in the things- that- will- probably- make- sense- later file, and forgot about it. She opened her legs wider to the spray of water, and came like you come in a wet dream.

Betsy handed Dallas a towel and hustled her out to the bending table, tapping her fingers as Dallas dried off and bent herself over. She pulled a chair up next to the table, and sat, and waited. Dallas waited with her, still a bit sleepy, puzzled but patient, happy to be bent over the magic table, wondering idly what was coming next.

The doorbell rang.

Dallas woke up, very suddenly, very thoroughly.

Betsy bounded to her feet and gave Dallas a reassuring pat on the butt. "Back in a sec," she said. Dallas froze, anything but reassured, as she heard the front door open and a clatter of voices and feet pour in. "You better have coffee, Betsy," one of the voices said. "Only you would schedule a gang bang for ten A.M. on a Monday." Dallas stayed frozen, all her senses on high alert. She kept her eyes focused straight ahead, her ears tuned to the murmuring in the kitchen. She heard a familiar voice among the chatter. "Hey, pumpkin," Jack said.

Dallas relaxed. Jack was here. She'd be okay. She smiled up at him as he took her chin in his hand. "It's good to see you, pie chart," he said. "It's been ages. Sheesh, you get a good piece of tail and you disappear off the planet. You never call, you never write..."

Dallas propped herself up on her elbows. "I know. I suck. How've you been? How's Bobby?" She peered over her shoulder, stealing her first anxious look at the group in the kitchen. "Is he here?"

"Nah. You know Bobby and girls. He's hopeless. If he saw a naked pussy, he'd probably die of shock. He said to say hi, though."

He stroked her hair as they chatted, and her breathing started returning to normal. He rested his hand on her shoulder as Betsy led the group in from the kitchen, and he pressed firmly as Dallas tensed up again. "Okay," Betsy said. "Everybody ready? Let's have some introductions." She quickly paraded the small group in front of Dallas's widening eyes. "Dallas, this is Roger, Ben, Lizzy, and Cheryl. Jack you already know. They're going to beat you and fuck you. Jack, you're already there, why don't you start us off?"

After that, things got a little strange.

She knew that Jack went first, knew it was his hand that moved from her shoulder and snaked down her spine and over her bottom. She knew that his second hand was joining the first, knew he was spreading her cheeks open, carefully examining her asshole, just as if he hadn't seen it a dozen times before.

And then... it wasn't a blur, it was much too clear for a blur, she knew every detail of what happened, but she could never remember later what came when, or in what order. Her libido was like a kid in a candy store, with a fifty-dollar bill and a free afternoon. Everywhere she turned, there was something to do, something to feel, something to pay attention to. Roger's cock was in her ass now, and if she lost interest in it even for a second, all she had to do was switch her attention, like changing channels, to Ben's hands gripping her wrists and pressing them into the table, or Cheryl's voice in her ear telling her how she was going to put Dallas's picture in the escort ads and pimp her out. Or she'd picture what she looked like, step back in her mind and watch herself get bent over and pinned down and buggered, like she was watching a dirty movie. And five minutes later, there'd be something else to do, to feel, to pay attention to. There was a blindfold over her eyes and her favorite vibrator between her legs, pulled away suddenly as a bamboo cane lashed down like lightning onto her ass; she screamed, and it all happened again, around in a circle: the sweet insistent buzzing between her legs, the quick moment of silence and stillness, the microsecond of blackout pain, the glowing afterburn on her ass, joining with the return of the buzzing on her clit to make her wriggle and whimper. Then the channel changed, and she was on the floor bent over a pile of pillows, her face buried in Jack's bare feet, breathing in his familiar scent, licking between his toes like they were vulvas. She saw Betsy move behind her, and she arched her back, getting ready for a finger or a paddle or God knows what; but Betsy just stood there watching, and Dallas smiled around Jack's toes, and writhed her ass for her lover like a peep-show dancer. Then the channel changed again, and a soft, semi-erect dick slipped into Dallas's mouth—Ben's, she thought, but she wasn't sure, she couldn't see his face, and she was starting to lose track of all the new names. The owner of the dick didn't pump her or move her head; he simply inserted his dick into her mouth and held it there, filling her mouth, sealing it shut. She sucked on it like a pacifier, like a bottle of whiskey.

And five minutes later, there'd be something else. There was always something else. Her world had turned into an enormous buffet dinner, elaborately prepared and perpetually restocked, her greed satisfied within moments of her noticing it. The easy stuff, like the bootlicking and the spankings, she gobbled up like potato chips; the hard stuff, like the deep throating and the push-ups and that god-awful stingy thing of Lizzy's, she shivered over and savored like good, fiery bourbon. At the same time her brain was getting confused, irritated with the effort of assimilating the input and trying to assign it meaning. She was crawling from person to person now, around in a circle again, nose to the floor, knees apart, begging each new person for some new indignity, saying words she had been told to say by the one before; kneeling behind Ben and begging to lick his asshole, begging Roger to ride her like a pony, spreading her asshole in front of Lizzy and begging her to whip it. They complied with her pleas, and she was exposed and humiliated; or they refused her pleas, and she was shamed and defeated. The argument in her body became strident, her brain saying "Enough already, call your fucking safeword"; her libido saying, "Not enough, not nearly enough, not yet."

After some amount of time, a practical voice swam to the surface and demanded attention, and she cleared her throat and asked for a pee break. Betsy untied her at once, took the buttplug from her ass, and led her to the bathroom. "Do you just need to pee, or do you need a break?" she asked.

"Huh?" Dallas mumbled, confused, inarticulate. "I have to pee. Can I pee?"

"Good," Betsy said. She guided Dallas into the bathtub. "Hands and knees," she said. "Wait." She called out to the living room. "Hey, guys, come on in." Dallas crumpled, as the group tromped into the bathroom and stood around the tub, watching, waiting. She was tired, she wanted to stop now, she wanted to curl up in the tub and cry herself to sleep. But she could feel another layer under the tears, something that wanted to stay, something that was quiet and soft and wanted to be seen. So she arched her back, and spread her knees so they could see, and peed in the tub, humiliated and peaceful. She was an animal in a zoo, a performer in the back room of a sleazy fucked-up whorehouse, and it didn't feel like make-believe, it felt real. She finished, kept her legs open, prayed that they would go home and leave her in peace, prayed that they would pet her and soothe her, prayed that one of them would smear an evil hand over her soaked clit. She felt Betsy's hand on her shoulder, and prayed that she'd keep it there forever.

Betsy rinsed her off, gently led her out of the tub, placed her on her knees on the floor, and then bent her over the toilet with a snap. Dallas drew a sharp moaning breath as Betsy grabbed her hair and wrapped it firmly around her hand. She could feel Betsy gesture with her other hand, could feel Jack coming up behind her, crawling between her knees, pressing his hard-on against the crack of her ass. Betsy held her there for a long minute, poised, savoring the moment. "Feel it," she murmured in Dallas's ear. "Feel it. This. Right now." Dallas shivered. She felt her knees grinding into the cold tile, her breasts shoved awkwardly against the rim of the toilet, the head of Jack's dick trembling at her asshole, Betsy's hand gripping her hair at the back of her head, her face hovering just above the toilet bowl. She was wide awake now. She held very still, seeing, feeling, listening. "Now," she heard Betsy say.

The hand on the back of her neck jerked down, pushing her head under the water, as Jack's dick pressed against her asshole and pushed its way inside. Her body fought hard against Betsy's hand, jerking and struggling, while she bucked back against Jack, arching her back, begging him with her body to fuck her harder. He took her hips in his hands and shoved into her, and Betsy yanked her head up out of the toilet and slapped her across her soaking wet face. Their eyes met. Dallas felt the joy radiating out of her face, saw it mirrored in Betsy's crazy eyes. Betsy shivered and dunked her again, and Dallas felt herself sinking into her body, her mind darting from the water in her nose to her scraped and sore knees, to the sweet, nasty stroking inside her delighted asshole, to her wet tangled hair, to the panic in her lungs, to the sudden gasp of air and the cracking of Betsy's hand across her drenched face. She could feel herself disappearing into her asshole, as Jack yanked his dick all the way out and slowly pushed it in again; then she was pulled abruptly back into her brain, as Betsy forced her head deep into the water and held it there with a shaking hand. The three of them came together, Jack shivering as he pressed a last stroke deep inside Dallas's asshole, Dallas screaming with Betsy as she dissolved into her lover's cruel hand and her friend's throbbing cock, Betsy feeling her orgasm on the palm of her hand as she screamed and delivered the final smack.

They all held very still for a long moment, peaceful, drifting, lost in the dark. They came back to life slowly, somewhat reluctantly, at the sound of applause. They had forgotten that the others were in the room.

There was a picnic dinner on Dallas's bed that evening, all seven of them, Dallas lying naked facedown in the middle, the others sitting cross-legged around her in various stages of undress. They ate cold chicken and apples and chocolate chips, and drank seltzer or beer, and congratulated themselves and one another on a job well done. Dallas was introduced again to her new friends, and she lazily began to sort them out a bit more clearly. Roger was the slender, blond, nerdy-cute one, who had fucked her in the ass again and again. Ben was the one with the curly black hair and the crude hands; she thought his dick was the stubby, veiny one, but it had gone soft now, so she couldn't be sure. Lizzy was the brunette with the strong arm and the boots and the scary, scary toys, and Cheryl had the red hair and the gravelly voice and the really fucked-up imagination. They all smiled at her now, and petted her, and stroked her with feathers and fur, and Jack got some sort of soothing gel out of the fridge and rubbed it onto her bottom, and she drifted off into a hazy half sleep while they ate and chatted around her. She woke as they were kissing her good-bye. Jack was the last to leave. "Call me," he said. "Let's talk soon."

She nodded. "I promise," she said. She fell back asleep to the sound of her friends being politely shooed out the door. She half woke in the middle of the night. Betsy had maneuvered the blankets out from under her and had tucked her in.

Day Four:

Dallas woke at six in the morning, Betsy's sleeping hand resting on her ass. She lay awake for several minutes, holding very still. Then she removed Betsy's hand and turned over onto her side. When Betsy stirred, she shook her. "Pretzel," she said.

"Hmrph?" mumbled Betsy, still asleep.

"Pretzel," Dallas repeated. "I'm done. I've had enough. Safeword." She snuggled against Betsy's wakening body. "Mmmmm," she purred. "Thank you so much. That was... mmmmmm. My God." She went back to sleep almost immediately, slept for hours, dreamed of clouds and food.

Betsy lay awake, staring at the ceiling. She stared for an hour or so. She read her book for a bit. She stared at the ceiling some more. She finally got back to sleep at about nine, and dreamed that someone was throwing slippers at her window.

They both woke at about noon.

"How are you doing?" Betsy asked.

"Fine," Dallas beamed. "Amazing. Just... wow. Can't explain, really." She pummeled Betsy lightly on the shoulder. "So what do you want to do today? We don't have anything planned. You wanna see a matinee or something? Do some shopping? Drive to Vegas? Throw paintballs at cigarette billboards?"

"I don't know," Betsy said hazily. "I'm not really here yet. Listen... do you want to... like, talk, or something? That was pretty intense. Do you want to talk about it?"

"Not really," Dallas replied. "I know it was a lot, but I actually feel fine. Relaxed, happy, not in any immediate need of processing. Mostly in immediate need of breakfast."

"Alright," Betsy said. She shrugged. "I guess you were right the first time. We didn't need two weeks after all."

"Nonsense," Dallas chirped. "It's good we had the time. It would have sucked, if we thought we had a deadline coming up. We would have felt rushed." She gave Betsy a loud, smacking kiss and bounced out of bed. "So, breakfast? Then what?"

They were waiting in line for the movie when Dallas did a double take. "Oh," she said. "God. Delayed reaction. I'm sorry. Do *you* want to talk about it?"

Betsy fiddled with her wristwatch. "That's okay," she said. "I mean, eventually, yes. But it doesn't have to be today. If you wanna see big special effects and stuff blowing up today, that's fine with me. You earned it. Ten times over."

"Aww," Dallas said. "That's sweet. But honestly, it's okay. If there's something else you'd rather do, I'm fine with that. I'm happy with pretty much anything right now."

She meant it, too. For the next several days, Dallas felt unusually calm, at peace with herself and the world. Her usual driving impatience had slipped off, and she was stopping in the middle of the sidewalk to look at trees, or sniff the fire in a nearby fireplace, or just notice that she was alive, here, in this place and time. People would smile at her as she passed, and she'd realize that she had been smiling, without knowing it, at nothing in particular. She was starting to get what those Zen idiots were talking about. She would stop in the middle of mundane events—shopping, reading, sorting laundry—and be filled with the immensity of the moment, the clear understanding that infinity and eternity were present in this minuscule sliver that was her life. Her thoughts wandered, curious and unhurried: food, dancing, illness, gardens, biology, conflict, death. Her thoughts visited these places, and were untroubled.

Except about sex.

It wasn't that her thoughts about sex were troubled. She just wasn't having many of them. Not in the usual way. She wasn't having masturbation fantasies, or fantasies that urged her to hurry off someplace where they could become masturbation fantasies. She wasn't really having fantasies of any kind. She was definitely thinking about sex at least some of the time, contemplating, philosophizing, reminiscing. She thought a lot about the last few days, and she smiled at the memories, which were lovely, salty and sweet, vastly entertaining. But the memories didn't drive her to the nearest private place to shove her hand down her pants. She would recall them happily, and then move on to the next thought.

For a bit. This was Dallas, after all. After a few days of calm, Zen-like, desire-free bliss, her clit began to wake up, stretch, shove off the blankets, and think about what it wanted to do that day. She was home alone when it started to twitch. The feeling was familiar and comforting, and with something of a sense of relief, she went over to her bed, bent over, pulled down her pants, and let her mind wander. She was a whore in an alley, bent over a garbage can with her skirt pulled up, a clumsy dick in her ass and a fifty-dollar bill in her mouth. She was in that damned mall on her hands and knees, scrabbling for her scattered belongings with her short skirt riding up over her panties. She was in a dingy basement tied to a rusty bed, spread-eagled on her back with a gag in her mouth, while a gang of fraternity boys lined up to—

She stopped. On her back? What the hell was that?

She shook her head and started again. She was in a dingy basement, bent over a rusty bed, her hands tied and a gag in her mouth, while the fraternity boys lined up. There, that was better. She moved on. She was a teenage Catholic schoolgirl bending over the Mother Superior's desk, pulling down her panties with hesitant hands. She was an exam subject in a cold white room, naked and shivering, flat on her back on a metal table—

She stopped again. Her hands jerked away from her clit like they'd been burned.

She'd had disturbing thoughts pop up in her fantasies before. Faces that she didn't want to think about that way—her boss, her mother, some of her more obnoxious exes—would occasionally slip into the stream of images that ran through her brain when she jerked off. It happened. She didn't like it, but she was used it, and she could generally shake off the images and move on to more comforting thoughts. But this... This was weird. Not weird, like walking up to your house at night and suddenly finding it unfamiliar. Weird, like walking up to your house at night and suddenly finding it gone.

She started again. She was on her back—

To hell with it. Something fucked up was going on, and she didn't want to deal with it. She stood up, jerked up her pants, stalked into the living room, and flipped on the TV.

The next day she was prepared. She pulled on a leather garter belt with black lace stockings and cowboy boots and no underwear, and a short tight black dress over it all. She cranked the bending table to its lowest point, to raise her ass up as high over her head as she could. She grabbed her vibrator, and her favorite hairbrushes, and a bottle of lube, and a series of buttplugs of various sizes, and plonked them all down within easy reach. She snapped herself over the bending table, pushed in the first buttplug, and started fantasizing.

She started with an old favorite. She was a prostitute at a party, hired as the evening's entertainment, bent over a crate on the dining room table, ready to take the crowd on one by one. The non-fantasy Dallas reached for the vibrator and shoved it between her legs. She was in no mood for teasy buildups—she wanted to come, now. The host at her fantasy party climbed up on the table and unzipped his fly... but then the party crowd rushed the table, they yanked the crate out from under her and flipped her onto her back, forcing her legs apart and straddling her face...

Dammit, dammit, dammit. No. She gritted her teeth. Maybe if she switched fantasies—something newer, less of a chestnut. Okay. She was at the leather street fair with Betsy, bent over with her hands pressed against a wall, with a sign Betsy had draped around her neck saying FREE TO ANYONE. A tall, ropy woman came over, said hi to Betsy, and with no introduction started smacking Dallas on the ass. She spun Dallas around, then pulled out a small flogger and aimed it at Dallas's breasts...

Dammit to fucking hell. Dallas jammed the vibrator hard against her clit. She squeezed her asshole tight around the buttplug, squeezed her eyes shut, and concentrated. Betsy and the tall ropy woman dragged her over to a nearby picnic table, bent her over it, and started smacking her ass. The real Dallas shoved her pelvis against the vibrator and focused grimly on the imaginary blows pounding her bottom. The tall woman suddenly grabbed Dallas by the hair and snarled in her ear. "On your back and spread your legs, slut—"

Oh, fuck it, Dallas thought. Fine. I'll just do it, this once. Whatever it is that's going on here, I'll see what it's about, and I'll get it over with.

She took a firmer grip on the vibrator and let the fantasy go where it wanted. Betsy and the tall ropy woman at the street fair hauled Dallas over to a picnic table and shoved her on her back. "Spread your legs, cunt," the tall woman snarled. "Spread them in front of all these people." The stranger pulled out a small flogger and aimed it between Dallas's legs...

Dallas came, hard, crying out. Her asshole clenched in spasms, her fingers gripped the vibrator until they hurt. She shivered, and came again, her fingers slippery from her juices, her mind filled with the image of her spread thighs and her open pussy, the strange woman whipping her between her legs, the crowd of strangers looking on. She shivered, and came again.

She stopped coming after a few minutes. She took a deep breath and slid the buttplug out of her ass. Well, she thought, that was interesting.

Not so bad. It's not like I died or anything. Maybe that'll be the last of it.

It wasn't the last of it.

The thoughts kept coming. She'd try to drive them off, or she'd try to distract herself, or she'd go ahead and jerk off to them. None of it made any difference. The thoughts were there. They'd tap her on the shoulder like an annoying coworker, or scream at her cheerfully like ads on TV. Whenever she masturbated. Then when she wasn't masturbating. Sexual images would drift into her head without warning, a phenomenon she was well used to by now, but now she found it distracting and disturbing. All that wonderful Zen-like bliss had dissolved, as if it had never been there, as if it had been a lie. She hadn't stepped away from the wheel at all; she was tied to it, and the wheel was on a roller coaster. She was excited and fluttered one hour, calm and curious the next, anxious and irritable the next. Until now, she had organized her entire sex life around being bent over. She had organized her life around it, period. Everything else had been built around it. But bending over was taking up less space in her mind every day, and in its place was this... hole. This enormous empty place where bending over used to be. And now her whole life was built around that empty place.

The thoughts kept coming. The first time she thought about tying up that cute bank teller and making him eat her pussy, she felt like crawling out of her skin. The third time she did it, she rolled her eyes and went on with her grocery shopping; the fifth time, she reached for her vibrator. Gradually, tentatively, the new fantasies were becoming less like strangers, and more like... not friends, but friendly acquaintances. But the very familiarity made her twitchy. It felt like it could be a trap.

When she started fantasizing about Betsy going down on her, she began to shake. She was at the movies, at a matinee, alone. She got out of her seat, hurried to the bathroom, and sat on the toilet, willing herself not to cry.

The next day, she told Betsy.

"No," Betsy said. "What? No."

Dallas's face fell. "So it's not okay."

"No," Betsy said. "It is not okay." She stood up and paced the room, agitated.

"So, you mean it's not okay with you, as in, you don't even want to try it?"

Betsy shook her head. "It's not okay with me, as in I don't want to try it. It's not okay with me that you want to try it. It's not okay with me that we're having this conversation. It is not okay with me, period, in any way. What the hell happened? What about those three days?" She blanched. "Oh, my God. Was it the three days? Did I take it too far? Did I really hurt you? Was it—"

"No," Dallas sighed. "The three days were... they were... Amazing. Mind-blowing. Really really good." She struggled for a moment for better words, then gave up. "It was the best thing, ever."

"So what the fuck?" Betsy asked. "How does something be the best thing ever, and then you don't want it anymore?"

Dallas shut her eyes. "I didn't say anymore. I didn't say I never want to get bent over again. I just want to try some other things, too." She opened her eyes and glared. "Anyway, why do I have to explain it? Since when do I have to explain to you why I want what I want?"

"Since you want me to go along with it," Betsy snapped. "Since I became a central part of your sex life. You don't get to just pull the rug out, and then set a bomb under the fucking floor, and not give me an explanation." She sat down, and immediately stood up and started pacing again. "Remember what your ad said? How you wanted to be bent over and done from behind, and you didn't want to do anything else? What the fuck is—"

"Yes, I remember," Dallas sighed again. "Of course I remember. But I didn't say forever, did I?"

Betsy stared as if she'd been slapped. Dallas pressed her advantage. "Do you want me to promise to always want the same things, and never want anything new, for the rest of my life? Do you think that's even remotely fair? Yes, I said I wanted to be bent over and done from behind, and I said I didn't want anything else. I didn't say I'd never want anything else ever. I didn't say I wanted to be bent over my wheelchair when I'm seventy, for fuck's sake. I want some new things now, and I don't think that's bad, and I'm not going to apologize for it. I'm not—"

"Don't get so fucking superior," Betsy snorted. "Like you've grown, expanded your horizons, and I'm still stuck in my immature, narrow-minded fetish."

Dallas threw her hands in the air. "I didn't say that. I don't think that. Don't put words in my mouth. Look, I just… Look. I know this is upsetting to you. It's upsetting to me, too. I didn't ask for it, I didn't expect it, I don't… And in answer to your question, I don't know what happened. Ever since those three days, it's been different. I've been different. Those three days, it was huge, way bigger than I expected, and that's not a slam at all, it was incredible, but it was a lot. Life-changing a lot. And life-changing things, they come out weird sometimes." She paused, scowling. "I don't know. We said we wanted to bend me over and do me until I had enough, and we did. I had enough."

"Well, I didn't," Betsy snapped. "I totally didn't have enough. I had ideas lined up for at least another week. Clear, detailed, planned-out ideas. Not to mention the stuff that was lurking on the back burner. I was really bummed that you called a halt when you did. I could have easily gone on for the whole two weeks. I wanted to."

Dallas sat silently for a long moment. "Jesus," she said at last. "I'm… God, I'm an idiot. That hadn't even occurred to me. I just assumed that after a couple of days, you'd mostly be doing it for my sake. I figured you'd get tired of it way before I did. I didn't—"

"What planet have you been on?" Betsy asked. "We've been doing this for, how long? Five months? What could possibly make you think I'd get tired of it? What do you think I've been doing all this time? Mercy fucks?" She clenched her hands, then carefully unclenched them. "Look. I just want to bend you over and do you from behind, and I don't want to do anything else. And I don't get why that's all of a sudden a problem."

"Okay," Dallas said "I get it. You don't want to do this. Fine. I'll just… I don't know. But you obviously don't want to do this, and I'm not going to try to argue you into it."

Betsy sat down, a bit calmer now. "Look. Why don't you do this other stuff with someone else? You know that's okay with me. I don't care if you fuck other people now and then. Run an ad or something. Get it out of your system."

"Maybe," Dallas said. "I guess that's a possibility. It's just..."

"It's just what?"

Dallas paused, choosing her words. "I don't know that it is going to be just every now and then. I don't know if I'm going to want to be bent over three or four times a week, and then go play on my back every month or two. That may not be enough. The way I feel now... maybe. I don't know yet."

Betsy stared. "Christ," she said. "I have no idea what to do with that information."

"Me, neither."

They sat for a moment. "Look," Betsy said at last. "I'm tired. You're tired. I don't think we're going to say anything else useful tonight. Let's go to bed. We'll talk more later."

They slept uneasily that night. They didn't see each other for a few days. When they did, they had the same fight again. Calmer, and with less cursing, but still the same. They met again the next day, and had the same fight yet again; calmer still, and with more "I'm sorry"s and "I know this is hard for you"s and "I really want you to be happy"s, but still the same.

Dallas called Jack that weekend.

"So how's Bobby?" Dallas asked. She set her teacup on his coffee table and plopped her feet up next to it.

"He's good," Jack said. "He's in Seattle this week. His sister just had a baby; he's helping her out." He paused for a moment. "We're talking about getting married, actually."

"Damn," Dallas said. "Who'da guessed. Well, good for you. Forsaking all others, and all that."

"Yeah, right," he snorted. "I don't think either of us is writing that one into our vows. More like 'Forsaking all others unless they're relatively sane and know not to mess with the relationship, in which case, go boff them already.' Anyway, we're just talking now. No decisions yet." He laughed. "Except for the caterers, of course. We haven't decided about kids yet, but we know we want dim sum."

Dallas groaned. "Sheesh. Californians. What will the wedding supper be? A steamed pork dumpling and a grilled snow pea?"

"You'll probably have barbecued ribs at yours," he retorted. "With pork chops on the side, and potato salad with bacon. Speaking of which, how are you and Betsy? Are wedding bells in the stars?"

Dallas scowled at her tea. "Come on," she mumbled. "We've been together, what, five months? Anyway... that's kind of what I wanted to talk to you about."

"Concerned face," Jack said. "Are you guys in trouble? You seemed so happy the last time I saw you."

"The last time you saw me, you had your dick in my ass. Of course I was happy."

"My dick doesn't make you that happy, muffin-chop. You were blissed. I've never seen you like that, and I've had my dick up your ass more than once. So what happened?"

"Well... it isn't her," Dallas said. "Not mostly. I'm..." She pulled at a lock of her hair. "You know how I only like the one thing in bed? How I just like to be bent over and done?"

Jack rolled his eyes.

"Screw you," Dallas grinned. "Anyway. I told you about our little sex vacation, how Betsy and I spent three days bending me over and doing me? The gang bang you were in, when you two had me over the toilet, that was part of that."

"Good times."

"Yeah. Well. Ever since then, I've been... there are these fantasies..." She stopped and stared at her teacup.

"Jesus," Jack said. "Spit it out. You want to get buggered by sheep? Gangbanged by the LAPD? Just tell me."

"Okay." Dallas took a deep breath. "I've been having fantasies about doing things, sexual things... that don't involve being bent over."

Jack raised his eyebrows, opened his mouth to speak, and closed it. He opened his mouth again, and left it hanging open.

"I know," Dallas replied. "I'm a freak of nature. But I'm serious. This is very weird for me. Ever since the three days with Betsy, I've been thinking about all these other... things. Being on my back. Strapping it on. I'm even thinking about topping, if you can believe it. All this shit I used to think was boring and pointless, now I can't stop thinking about it. All the fucking time. I mean, I still think about being bent over, but only now and then. Ever since those three days."

Jack nodded. "Interesting. You found the Holy Grail, and it turned out the Grail wasn't what you wanted after all."

"No," she sighed. "No, no, no, no, no! That is most emphatically not what I meant at all. It was exactly what I wanted. It was... It wasn't like, you got the Grail, but it turns out the Grail sucks. It was like, you got the Grail, and the Grail is amazing, but then what?"

Jack chuckled. "Have you read the scripts for *Monty Python and the Holy Grail?*" Dallas shook her head. "Very funny," he said. "I'll lend you the book sometime. Anyway, in one of the earlier drafts, the Knights find the Holy Grail, very cool, they're very happy. And then they stand around for a bit, kind of dissatisfied, wondering what to do next. And then they decide that one of them should hide the Grail, so they can all go looking for it again."

Dallas laughed. "Yeah. That. But in a way, it's just the opposite. It wasn't unsatisfying at all. It was... All those years of being bent over, it was never enough. Nobody else wanted it like I did, so I always just grabbed what I could get. Like not knowing where my next meal was coming from." She shrugged one shoulder. "Now I know. I can have enough of it. So I can relax. I can want other things. And I do."

"So what's the problem?" he asked. "I've known you for what, two years? Two and a half? And you've never not wanted to want something before. Not in bed, anyway. What's the deal?"

"Well—Betsy, for one," she said. "And for two, and for three. She is seriously not okay with this. We may not survive it." She looked down at her hands. "I never got this before, but she's into the whole bending over thing even more than I was. She has been, all along. And our little vacation didn't change her mind. I think it actually made her want it more. She got the Grail, and now she's like, 'Cool, amazing, where can I get some more grails?'" She rubbed her eyes. "I feel awful. She gave me this amazing gift, and I take it and say, 'That's great, sweetie, thank you ever so much, now here's what I want tomorrow.' I suck. I can't even—"

"No," he said. "Shut up. Look, there may be things about you that suck, but trust me, wanting the kind of sex you want is not one of them." He shrugged. "You guys just want different things now."

"So what do we do about it?"

"Beats me. Look, I hate to sound harsh, but you do about it what every other couple in the free world does when they have serious differences. You compromise, or you suck it up and live with it, or you break up. This isn't the movies—being honest and brave and true to your heart doesn't guarantee you a happy ending. You can make all the right choices, and things will still suck sometimes." He patted her hand, trying to be comforting; he looked at her downcast face, and abruptly changed the subject. "So, just to be clear. These fantasies you're having, they're not just things that are fun to think about when you whack off? They're things you want to do, with your actual body?"

"God," she sighed. "That's the question before the court, isn't it? If I knew that... Well, yeah. I guess I want to at least try them. With my actual body. If for no other reason than to find out."

He nodded. "So are you propositioning me?"

Dallas was suddenly derailed, her mind pulled from its philosophical wanderings to the here and now. "Huh?" she said. "Oh. No. I was just saying..." She looked at Jack, and her mind shifted over onto yet another rail, a friendly and happy and enticing rail. "But... well, now that you mention it—"

Jack laughed, a deep, friendly belly laugh. "You are so easy," he said. "I completely adore how easy you are. You are the least coy person I know. I have never known you to even think about saying no when you want to say yes." He put his teacup down. "Now?"

Dallas hesitated, still somewhat derailed. But she was adjusting rapidly to the new track. "Sure," she said. "Why the hell not. No gift like the present."

"Good," he said. He strolled over behind her chair, gave her shoulders a quick massage, and sneakily began to play with her breasts.

Her breasts.

Now, that was interesting. Novel. For some years now, her breasts had been pretty much out of commission, mushed up against a bed or a table for the most part, or else dangling uselessly in the air, in front of a sawhorse or some such thing. Oh, they sometimes got clamps put on them, or were fumbled with blindly for a few moments from behind. But now Jack was circling in on them, patient, relaxed, completely focused, like they held the secret to perfect happiness and he had all the time in the world to find it, and Dallas was starting to think that he might not be wrong about that. He spent long, lazy minutes cupping and massaging the curves of her breasts through the fabric of her T-shirt, and another slow minute pulling her T-shirt up to her armpits, lingering as he drew the hem across her nipples and exposed them to the air. Dallas felt her nipples stiffen. She glanced down self-consciously to see what they looked like.

Jack began playing a bit more seriously now, tracing his fingers from the outer rim of her curves to a micron away from her nipples, then back out again, like a postulant walking a labyrinth. He teased her, pleasantly, nastily, circling his fingers around her nipples as if they might explode if he touched them too soon. Dallas squirmed and slumped back in her chair; she felt awkward, self-conscious, and Jack's sadistically patient fingers were making her feel decidedly off balance. But they were also making her feel like she'd crumble into dust if he didn't touch her nipples in the next six seconds. Jack purred; he always loved making her beg for it, whether it was with her words or her body, and she was begging for it now, letting out little whimpering moans and shoving her breasts out as far as she could. He took pity and brushed his fingertip over one nipple; Dallas wailed, and ground her hips in panicked circles into the hard seat of her chair. Her mind drizzled out of her head and distilled itself into her nipples, paying frantic attention to every spiral and brush, every millimeter of pressure and movement. At the same time, she felt a sort of calm curiosity, an inner watcher taking notes for future reference. Her nipples felt like clitorises, a bit less sensitive but capable of tolerating more, which might be useful. Especially now that Jack was pinching them. He squeezed them slowly like a gradually tightening vise, and let go sharply. And again, a bit harder each time, like a rising tide. She held her breath with each pinch, fighting the pain and then relaxing and letting it in, then letting it all rush out in a huge sigh of relief when he let go.

He squeezed her nipples then, hard, and twisted them hard, and didn't let go this time. He twisted them harder, a sharp, vicious twist, digging his fingers in deep, and she screamed, and pounded her feet on the floor, and felt a spasm shake her body from her shoulders to her belly. It was over in a second. The sensation in her nipples quickly shifted from painful to annoying, and she knocked Jack's hands away, and then grabbed them and pressed the palms flat against her breasts.

"Jesus," she gasped. She wasn't sure what the hell that was. It wasn't quite an orgasm, or maybe it was. It was fading quicker than a regular orgasm, or maybe her brain was just rushing in faster than usual to process the new information. She looked up at Jack and smiled, suddenly self-conscious again. "Hello, sailor," she said.

"Hey, little lady," he replied. "How you doing?"

"Good," she said. "Weird, but good. I'd do it again." She scowled. "But now I feel all awkward. I don't know what comes next."

"Well, we can give it a minute," he said. "I'm sure you'll think of something." He went into the bathroom to pee.

"So how was it for you?" she called through the door.

"Great," he replied. "Different. It's nice to see your face when you're coming. You really get lost, it's gorgeous to look at." He laughed. "I always did think you were a better fuckbuddy than you were a lover."

Her back stiffened. She sat up rigidly and pulled her T-shirt back down over her breasts. "What do you mean?"

"Well, you know," he said. "You were a bit of a black hole when we were lovers. Not really a black hole, it's not like you didn't give anything back, but you were awfully obsessed with your little obsession. If we weren't doing your thing, you weren't really in the room. You were pretty much..." He came back into the living room, looked at her face, and stopped. "What?"

She was staring at him, alarmed, pissed, her arms crossed over her belly. "You think I'm a black hole?"

"No," he sighed. "I specifically said you weren't. I wouldn't have stuck it out for three months if you were. It's just, what I wanted always felt like this... annoyance. To you, I mean. Except when it dovetailed with what you wanted. I always felt kind of irrelevant." He looked seriously at her stricken face and sat down. "Dallas, you're not an idiot. You must know all this, right? Don't tell me this is just now occurring to you."

She glared at her hands, irritated, queasy, silent. She stayed silent for some time. "What did you want that you weren't getting?" she finally said.

"Well," he shrugged, "some actual submission might have been nice. You know, that whole 'My deepest pleasure is to serve your desire, your merest whim drives the whole of my being' thing. And... well, you might have thought about doing me every once in a while. I'm not always Mister Super-Tough Top Guy. I like to take it sometimes."

She stared at him as if his skin had peeled back, revealing itself to be nothing more than a clever disguise. "You like to take it?"

"Sometimes."

She kept staring. "You like to get done."

He nodded, patiently, kindly, as if he were talking to a slow five-year-old. "Yes, Dallas," he said. "I like to get done."

His tone irritated her. "Fine," she snipped. "Mister Super-Tough Top Guy. How about now."

"Now?"

"Sure. Why the hell not. Now."

The last word came out sharper than she intended—less like a suggestion, more like an order. "Yes, ma'am," he said sardonically. "At your service."

"Fine," she replied. "Into the bedroom." She snapped her fingers and pointed.

He met her eyes, dubious, concerned. "You're not kidding."

She looked meaningfully at her pointed finger, then looked back at him.

"You're certain about this?" he asked.

Now that he wasn't being an asshole, she wasn't certain at all. She kept pointing and stayed silent, afraid that if she said anything, even a short word like "yes," her voice would crack and call her a liar. She followed Jack as he shrugged and walked into the bedroom, and settled herself cross-legged on his bed, her back stiff, wondering the hell she was going to do now. Jack stood in the middle of the room facing her calmly, smiling, waiting. "Now strip," she said. She sounded pissed. Jack stopped smiling, dropped his eyes, and slowly pulled his T-shirt over his head. He bent over to take off his shoes. "Turn around when you do that," Dallas snapped.

He stopped. They looked at each other, awkward, nervous, suddenly unfamiliar. Jack was less arrogant now; he was playing anxiously with his belt loops, and Dallas began to panic. If I want to back out of this, Dallas thought, now's the time.

They held each other's gaze. He tilted his head inquisitively, a gesture she'd seen him make a hundred times, and she let out a deep breath as she recognized him again. It was just Jack. This would be okay. She grinned at him broadly, and he grinned back, relieved. "While we're young," she said.

Jack blushed, and turned away from her. He bent over to untie his sneakers, and Dallas watched the small, compact curve of his ass swell through the fading denim. Okay, this is weird, she thought. But it doesn't suck. He stood up again, topless and barefoot, and she hopped off the bed and led him over to it.

"Now bend over," she commanded. "Bend over and pull down your pants."

It was weird as hell, saying those words herself. Hearing them come out of her own mouth. But they still had the punch. She was just on the other side of it. She could see the words land in Jack's head, could see the squirming in his belly as he fumbled with his fly, and it echoed inside her own belly. She felt a flash of jealousy as he dropped his jeans to his ankles, jealousy that quickly turned to cruelty and a desire to make him squirm even more. "Step out of them," she ordered. "I want you totally nude."

He hesitated for a second, and she slapped him on the ass. He flinched, and complied, kicking his pants away and slowly stretching out in front of her. She bit her lip. In all the times they'd played, she'd never seen him completely naked before. He had a nice body, with wiry legs and a thin, strong back. It was a pleasure to look at, and it suddenly struck her that she could have that pleasure for as long as she wanted. She didn't have to wait, didn't have to sit through fumblings and bad guesses, didn't have to hope that he'd pick up her signals. She could have anything she wanted from him, the moment she wanted it. She could have her own custom-made dirty movie, in the flesh, for her eyes and her hands and her pussy only, just by opening her mouth. She was suddenly impatient. "Spread your legs," she ordered.

His fingers twitched as he obeyed. She opened his bedside drawer and scrambled through it clumsily, scattering the rejects on the bed. She stripped down and spent a frustrating minute fiddling with the dildo harness, tripping as she stepped into it, then struggling into a pair of latex gloves. She sighed with relief and looked over at Jack. His body was relaxing, not in a good way but in a bored way; he was slumped over the bed, looking like he might start drumming his fingers any minute, and his hard-on had dropped an inch or two. Oops, she thought. She cleared her throat. "Spread them wider, and arch your back," she growled. "Show it off." She was immediately embarrassed at herself, she couldn't believe she'd resorted to such a chestnut; but he wasn't used to being on display like this, and he slipped back into shame and submission in the moment he complied. Her embarrassment slipped off into a dark corner to mutter to itself, and her impatience returned, restless and annoyed at having been kept waiting. She lubed up her finger, and slipped it in.

He sighed as she fingered him, giving something up, letting something else in, reaching towards her with his ass to beg for more. She quickly slid a second finger in, urgent, curious, in a hurry to get where she was going. She swirled the dildo at the rim of his asshole, and pushed it in.

The rhythm of her hips and the dildo's pressure on her clit was lovely, and it was frustrating, winding her up like a toy and not letting her go. Her mind scrambled, searching for a foothold, taking a step backward to look around. She saw the bedroom littered with toys and smelling of sex; she saw her beautiful naked friend bent over his bed, squirming and digging his fingers into the blankets; she saw herself, her breasts jiggling, the straps of the harness digging into her ass, her long slender cock disappearing into Jack and then reappearing like magic. The picture in her head pushed her up the ladder, tickling the clit in her brain. "Jerk yourself off," she snapped.

The command in her voice startled them both. She felt it as a strength in her shoulders and a snarl in her jaw; he felt it like a rope around his chest that made his heart soften and his dick stiffen, and he reached obediently between his legs and started stroking, propping himself up as best he could on one elbow. His awkwardness and obedience fascinated her, made her ravenous. "Jerk off, cunt," she snarled. "Mister Tough Top-Guy."

An idea flashed into her brain. She kept her hips moving while she scrambled through the toys on the bed. In the jumble of leather and whatnot, she found a small, dick-shaped dildo. "Take that," she snapped, thrusting it in front of Jack's face. "Fuck yourself in the mouth with it. Jerk off with one hand, and fuck your mouth with the other. I'd do it, but I'm busy." He complied immediately, and she twisted her fingers into his hair and pulled his head back hard, eager to hurt him, eager to see the dildo pumping into his mouth. His face was flushed, contorted around the dildo; he was clearly embarrassed, and just as clearly relishing the embarrassment. His blissful greed was so familiar to her; she suddenly knew what she looked like, what Betsy and Jack and dozens of others had seen when they worked her over. It was gorgeous: artless, fragile, stubborn. It was enormous. Her eyes widened, and then twitched: it was too much, she couldn't think about it right now. She abruptly pulled the dildo out of Jack's asshole and started smacking his ass with her lubey hand. "Squirt into your hand," she snapped. "Now." He gave himself three hard strokes and came, moaning incoherently around the dildo in his mouth. She shut her eyes and kept hitting him, hit him until her hand hurt, until he was whimpering and shaking and clawing the sheets. Sweet Jesus, she thought. What the fuck am I doing? She pulled back her hand midstroke, coming back to earth with a splattering thud. She started caressing his ass with a light, tickling touch. "Hey," she said anxiously.

He turned over and grinned up at her. His face was vague and stupid and happy, like he'd been eating chocolate and drinking cheap whiskey. "Hey," he replied.

She drew a huge sigh of relief, and he grinned wider. "So, do you have your answer?" he smirked.

She smiled back, a sardonic vampire-lizard smile. "What do you think?"

"I'm serious. I wanna know. Is this the new Dallas, or is it just a passing fad?"

She wriggled out of the harness and sat down on the bed. "No, I don't have my answer. Bits of one, maybe. It was great, though. Judges give it a nine- point- seven. If that's what you're asking."

"It wasn't," he said. "But thanks."

She shrugged uncomfortably and changed the subject. "So how was it for you?"

"Damn," he said. "Lovely. Weird." She was looking at him intently, and he coughed and averted his eyes. "You know this doesn't... you and I aren't..." He looked down, scowling, not as if he couldn't find words, but as if he knew the words and didn't want to say them.

"Oh!" Dallas rolled her eyes. "No. No no no. Don't worry about that. That ship sailed long ago. This is just us. Just friends." She patted his hand. "Special friends."

"Good," he sighed, and squeezed her hand. "So, friend. I have an idea."

"Uh-oh. That sounds dangerous. Famous last words."

He stuck out his tongue. "Remember how I used to smack your pussy and make you beg to be bent over?" he asked.

"Duh. Of course I remember. That's not the sort of thing a girl forgets."

"Well, now I want to play another game," he said. "Sort of like that one." He dug through the pile of toys on the bed and pulled out a slender metal ruler. "Here's how it goes. I'm going to smack your pussy, and you're going to beg for whatever pops into your head. Whatever you want most at that moment, beg me for it. You want twenty different things, beg me for all of them." He caressed the ruler and smacked it against his palm. "I should tell you now, I'm not going to promise to do all of them. I'm not even going to promise to do any of them. I just want to hear you to say them." He stopped fiddling with the ruler. "Is this okay? Do you want to play?"

She chuckled. "You should have been a shrink. Yeah, sure. I'm game."

She shoved the pile of toys to one side, flopped back on the bed, and opened her legs, grinning. She felt oddly curious; she'd certainly been on her back with her legs spread before, but she'd never wanted to be there, and she'd always flipped herself over in her mind so she could get off. Now she sprawled back luxuriously and opened her legs, savoring the anticipation, and the novelty of it. Jack pushed her knees up and apart, and she gave a startled yelp. She was used to feeling exposed; she'd had her clothes and defenses and dignity stripped and tossed aside more times than she could name. But she wasn't used to having her face exposed along with her goodies. Her face felt like an open book, a cheap trashy paperback porno with her wet pussy and throbbing clit right there on the first page. She looked up anxiously to meet Jack's eyes, but his gaze was firmly fixed between her legs.

He picked up the ruler and started tapping her between her legs, a steady rhythm like a heartbeat. Lightly, then a little less lightly. "Start talking," he said. "Start begging. I'm listening. Tell me what you want."

"I want..." She went silent. What the hell did she want? This was so good, so sweet, this, what he was doing right now. She guessed she should say so. "Please, sir," she mumbled. "Please keep spanking my pussy. Please spank my pussy with your ruler." She warmed to her subject as the sharp blows stayed steady on her swelling lips and exposed clit. "Please, sir, please make me spread my legs so you can hurt me, please hit my pussy, hurt it, please."

The pain on her clit was a bit harder now, and her mind darted away from it and raced around her body. She felt empty. Where did she feel empty? She licked her lips, and started begging again. "Please, sir. Please let me suck your cock. Please, sir, force it in, slap me in the face and hold my head still and shove your cock down my throat. Oh, God, please..." Her mind shifted. "I want your balls now, sir. I want to stick out my tongue and lap your balls like a dog, I want you to call me a cocksucking whore while you dangle them in my face and make me beg to suck them, I want you to—"

"Beg me," he snapped. "You're not begging. You're telling me. Beg me. Cunt." He smacked her pussy hard, a single sharp, cruel stroke that wiped out her words and brought tears to her eyes. He returned to the steady, painful-but-tolerable smacking.

"I'm sorry," she whimpered. "You're right, sir. Please forgive me. Please, sir." She gasped for air and groped, as her mind filled up and started leaking. "Please, sir, oh God, please straddle my face and stick your balls into my mouth, and please spread my legs and whip my pussy. Please make me lick your asshole, please pin me down and grind your asshole into my face while you spread my legs and whip me."

Her mind was crawling all over her body, groping from place to place like the hands in her gang-bang fantasies. "Please, sir, please fuck my tits, pinch them till they're raw and then shove them together, please slap my face while you shove your dick between my sore tits and fuck them. I'm begging you, take me out on the street and bend me over a garbage can and pull my pants down and stick a dildo in my ass, right on the street. Please, sir. Please do it, right in the middle of the day, please bend me over and stick a dildo in my ass so everyone can see. Please, I'm begging you, I need it, please take off your belt and beat me and make me crawl down the sidewalk with a dildo up my ass."

He turned the volume up a notch, keeping the relentless heartbeat rhythm but striking with a sharper hand. Her eyes rolled back, and she started breathing in ragged shudders. Usually when she took a beating, the pain and pleasure were separated, even if just by a tenth of a second;

there was the lovely fear and trembling just before, and then the tenth of a second of pain itself, which was in fact painful and kind of sucked, and then the sweet burning high just after, all in sequence, lined up like ducks in a row. But now the pain and pleasure were immediate, superimposed, the wires perfectly crossed, the strands not just twisted together but fused. Her words trailed off into babbling, and she went silent, slipping gently into the electrified darkness. He smacked her hard again, bringing her back with a jolt. "Keep talking," he said.

She took a deep gasp of air, and continued. "Please, sir. Please keep hitting me. Sweet Jesus, please don't stop." Her words came roaring back, a fire in an oil refinery, a souped-up race car driven by a lunatic. "Please, sir," she jabbered. "Please, I want you to take me to a sex party, one of the skanky ones with all the single straight guys pulling on their dicks, and I want you to make me be a party favor. Please make me lie on my back and spread my legs and let my pussy get fucked by every one of those guys. Except the ones who straddle my face, straddle me and stick their cocks in my mouth and fuck my face until I can hardly breathe. Please, sir, make me be the cocksucking pussy who lets herself get used by all the guys at the party who can't get laid." She shuddered, and kept talking, Jack's ruler driving the words out of her pussy and up out of her mouth. "Please, sir, find me a girl and bend her over the bed, and shove me down on my knees behind her and make me lick her asshole. Please spread her cheeks for me sir, put your fingers right up next to her asshole and spread it wide and make me lick it clean." She whimpered, and kept talking, the words pushing and bumping against each other, fighting each other to get out first. "Please, sir, please make me spread my legs and then piss on my clit, please pin me on my back and piss in my mouth, please force your cock in my mouth, pull my hair and hold my head and shove it in and make me cry, please bend me over and spread my cheeks and make me beg you to spank my asshole, please make me grovel on the floor and spread my pussy with my hands while I lick your shoes, please make me lie on my back and finger myself while you slap me, beat me, my pussy, my mouth, force me, fuck me, my asshole, spread my asshole, my clit, please..."

She was babbling now, the images tumbling through her mind too fast for her words to keep up. She felt turned inside out, her asshole and pussy and breasts and mouth and clit all exposed, all beaten, all fucked, all at once. Her legs shook and spasmed as she tried to spread them wider. Her mind swirled through her body, and then circled in tightly onto her clit, where Jack's ruler was spanking her harder, as hard as she could take it, no harder, trying to make her take it for as long as she could. All she could feel now was her clit, sore, raw, hungry for comfort, hungry for more pain. "My clit," she said. "Please, sir. My clit. Please."

"What?" he asked. "Tell me. Beg me. I'm listening. What do you want?"

"Please, sir," she gasped. "Do something. Please. Stroke it, pinch it, rub it... something... please..."

He dropped the ruler at once and reached between her legs. She came at the first touch of his hand, came in a spasm that jerked her belly tight and curled her up into a ball. She kept coming as he kept his hand in place, the spasms moving up into her chest, into her throat, into her face like sobbing, and out through the top of her head.

She took a deep breath, and came again. Peaceful this time, the pleasure spreading quietly through her veins and into her muscles like an I.V. The Zen-like bliss she'd lived with for such a short time came back now, drifting back into her chest like it was coming home. It had a different flavor this time: looser, foamier, less like morphine, more like laughing gas. The words and pictures that had spilled out of her hung in the air, and she arched her back and let them sink into her belly and burrow into her bones. She breathed, long, deep breaths like her lungs were bursting out of metal bands, and kept coming, or doing something that was very much like coming, not shaking or stabbing her this time, just lifting her gently, a glider in the night sky.

It lasted a long time. Jack's fingers stayed on her clit, pressing, shifting, circling slowly, as she slowly drifted back to earth and settled back into her body.

She opened her eyes when she was done. Jack was smiling at her, a little wistfully, stroking her thigh. "So," he said.

"So," she replied. She had her answer. Like a magic 8-ball: all signs point to yes. She curled up in her friend's arms, and started to cry.

Resource Guide

I said this in the introduction, but I'll say it again: This book is not a how-to guide on safe, consensual sadomasochism and kinky sex. This is a book of fantasies. While some of the stories here describe reasonably safe and healthy kinky relationships, many of them absolutely do not. The stories here are meant to entertain, to arouse, to provoke thought, to provide insight, to provide sexy images for you to get off on while you fuck or play or diddle yourself. But they are not meant to be replicated in real life. (Except in a consensual, safe, negotiated, acting- out-fantasies way.)

So what do you do if you *do* want information on how to practice safe, consensual sadomasochism and kinky sex?

Here are some resources to help you out. It includes books, websites, hotlines, and discussion forums, with information and ideas on how to navigate real-world SM safely—both physically, and emotionally.

You may or may not want to do SM in your real life. Lots of people have kinky fantasies that they have no interest in acting out. And that's totally fine. But lots of people have kinky fantasies that they're very interested in acting out. And that's totally fine, too. If that's you, and you don't know how to get started—or if you've already gotten started, and you want some ideas about how better to do what you're doing or how to take it further—here are some resources to help you out. Have fun!

HOTLINES

San Francisco Sex Information, http://sfsi.org/. A hotline and FAQ of free, confidential, accurate, non-judgmental information about sex. Including, but not limited to, kinky sex and SM. They answer questions by phone and email, and have a website with answers to frequently asked questions.

BOOKS

150 Shades Of Play: A Beginner's Guide To Kink, by Em and Lo

Bondage For Sex, Volume 1, by Chanta Rose

The Compleat Spanker, by Lady Green

Consensual Sadomasochism : How to Talk About It and How to Do It Safely, by William A. Henkin and Sybil Holiday

Erotic Bondage Handbook, by Jay Wiseman

Family Jewels: A Guide to Male Genital Play and Torment, by Hardy Haberman

Flogging, by Joseph W. Bean

Health Care Without Shame: A Handbook for the Sexually Diverse and their Caregivers, by Charles Moser, PhD, MD

How to Be Kinkier: More Adventures in Adult Playtime, by Morpheous

How to Be Kinky: A Beginner's Guide to BDSM, by Morpheous

Intimate Invasion: The Erotic Ins and Outs of Enema Play, by M. R. Strict

Leathersex: A Guide For The Curious Outsider And The Serious Player, by Joseph W. Bean

The New Bottoming Book, by Dossie Easton and Janet Hardy

The New Topping Book, by Dossie Easton and Janet Hardy

Play Piercing, by Deborah Addington

Playing Well With Others: The Kink, Leather, and BDSM Communities, by Lee Harrington and Mollena Williams

The Seductive Art of Japanese Bondage, by Midori and Craig Morey

The Sexually Dominant Woman: A Workbook for Nervous Beginners, by Lady Green

Slavecraft: Roadmaps for Erotic Servitude, by a grateful slave, with Guy Baldwin, M.S.

SM 101: A Realistic Introduction, by Jay Wiseman

Two Knotty Boys Back On the Ropes, by Two Knotty Boys and Ken Marcus

Two Knotty Boys Showing You the Ropes: A Step-By-Step, Illustrated Guide for Tying Sensual and Decorative Rope Bondage, by Two Knotty Boys and Larry Utley

The Toybag Guide to Age Play, by Lee Harrington

The Toybag Guide to Basic Rope Bondage, by Jay Wiseman

The Toybag Guide to Canes and Caning, by Janet W. Hardy

The Toybag Guide to Clips and Clamps, by Jack Rinella

The Toybag Guide to Dungeon Emergencies and Supplies, by Jay Wiseman

The Toybag Guide to Erotic Knifeplay, by Miranda Austin and Sam Atwood

The Toybag Guide to Foot and Shoe Worship, by Midori

The Toybag Guide to High-Tech Toys, by John Warren

The Toybag Guide to Hot Wax and Temperature Play, by Spectrum

The Toybag Guide to Medical Play, by Tempest

The Toybag Guide to Playing With Taboo, by Mollena Williams

The Ultimate Guide to Kink: BDSM, Role Play, and The Erotic Edge, by Tristan Taormino

Wild Side Sex: The Book of Kink, by Midori

Acknowledgments

First, last, and always: Ingrid.

Susie Bright has helped me more than I can say: not just with this book, but with the entire arc of my writing career. I cannot begin to thank her enough. But I'll try. Thanks.

Many thanks to David Fitzgerald, Ben Gamble, and Chris Hall, for reading early drafts of the book and giving me feedback. Even when I rejected their advice, it was extremely useful in helping me think things through. (And it's good to know that the unicorn story worked.)

One of the downsides of being married to a writer is that you get drafted into unpaid duty as copy editor and proofreader. Many thanks, therefore, go once again to Ingrid, for her patience and good humor with this process. Reading porn for typos, grammatical errors, and continuity cannot be easy. I hope at least that it was fun.

Thanks to my cover designer, Casimir Fornalski. He gets it.

Thanks to Amy and Rob Siders at 52 Novels for their excellent work on formatting the e-book.

And last, first, and always: Ingrid.

About the Author

Greta Christina has been writing about sex for over two decades, for publications including Ms., Penthouse, On Our Backs, and three volumes of Best American Erotica. She is author of Why Are You Atheists So Angry? 99 Things That Piss Off the Godless, an Amazon best-seller in the Atheism category, and is one of the most widely-read and well-respected bloggers in the atheist blogosphere. She blogs at the cleverly named Greta Christina's Blog, which was ranked by an independent analyst as one of the Top Ten most popular atheist blogs, and her writing has appeared in numerous magazines, newspapers, and anthologies, including Salon, AlterNet, and the Chicago Sun-Times. She is editor of the Best Erotic Comics anthology series and of Paying For It: A Guide by Sex Workers for Their Clients. She has been writing professionally since 1989, on topics including sexuality and sex-positivity, atheism and skepticism, LGBT issues, politics, culture, and whatever crosses her mind. She is on the speakers' bureaus of the Secular Student Alliance and the Center for Inquiry. She tweets at @GretaChristina. She lives in San Francisco with her wife, Ingrid.